"You think someone was in here?"

"I think chances are very good that the shadow you saw in the store was human, not imaginary, and our arrival interrupted whoever was going through your stuff, Chancy."

"But why?"

"I don't know. I do think you should notify the sheriff, though."

"And tell him what, Nate? He sounded pretty miffed when I told him we'd found the stolen van ourselves."

"It's his job to check out possible crimes. At least you can ask him to keep an eye on your store for you during the night."

That suggestion made Chancy laugh nervously. "I don't think that would help. Nobody is actually on duty from midnight to six in the morning."

"I don't believe this place. What about crime?"

"There isn't any to speak of," she answered.

"Wrong," Nate said sternly. "Now there is."

VALERIE HANSEN

was thirty when she awoke to the presence of the Lord in her life. In the years that followed her turn to Jesus she worked with young children, both in church and secular environments. She also raised a family of her own and played foster mother to a wide assortment of furred and feathered critters.

Married to her high school sweetheart since age seventeen, she now lives in an old farmhouse she and her husband renovated with their own hands. She loves to hike the wooded hills behind the house and reflect on the marvelous turn her life has taken. Not only is she privileged to reside among the loving, accepting folks in the breathtakingly beautiful Ozark mountains of Arkansas, she also gets to share her personal faith by telling the stories of her heart for Steeple Hill's Love Inspired line.

Life doesn't get much better than that!

VALERIE HANSEN
Shadow of Turning

Steeple
Hill®

Published by Steeple Hill Books™

STEEPLE HILL BOOKS

Steeple
Hill®

ISBN-13: 978-0-373-44247-8
ISBN-10:   0-373-44247-5

SHADOW OF TURNING

www.SteepleHill.com

Printed in U.S.A.

Every good gift and every perfect gift is from above, and cometh down from the Father of Lights, with whom is no variableness or shadow of turning.
—*James* 1:17

I actually am a certified
"Severe Weather Storm Spotter"
thanks primarily to my husband's urging
and equal participation in the class.

This book is dedicated to him.

PROLOGUE

"You did *what* with them?"

The thin young woman gripping the telephone receiver cowered even though the man on the other end of the line was behind bars and miles away. "I didn't know they were so important, Sam. They were just a bunch of old keys in a drawer. How was I supposed to know any of them mattered?"

"If they were mine, they mattered," he shouted. "Get them back, all of them, you hear."

"I'll—I'll try."

"You'd better do more than try," he said with evident menace. "You'd better have every one of those keys in your hand and be waiting for me when I get out of here in sixteen more days or you'll never do another one of those idiotic craft pictures of yours— or any other kind."

"They're three-dimensional collages," she replied, sniffling. "I've sold quite a few of them and it's a good thing, too, or I'd've starved waiting for you to serve your time. I don't know why you couldn't have just told them what they wanted to know and cut a deal."

"Plea bargain?" He cursed colorfully. "Not on your life. I kept my mouth shut for a reason and you had the keys to my future—to *our* future—until you lost them."

"But which ones do you want? How will I tell?" She began to sob. "Oh, Sam, honey, I'm so sorry."

"Shut up. Pull yourself together and think."

"I will. I promise. I only used the keys in three or four pictures and I'm pretty sure I remember who bought them. If they won't sell them back to me I'll do whatever I have to do to get my hands on them. I promise."

"You'd better," he rasped. "I'm not the only one who's counting on you. My partners aren't nearly as softhearted as I am. Understand?"

Nodding, she bid him a tearful goodbye, ran to the shoe box where she kept her receipts and dumped its contents onto her bed where she could spread everything out.

Her fingers flew through the papers, scattering them like dry leaves in a gale. Three pink receipts stood out as possibilities and she plucked them from the jumble. Two of those sales had been to furniture stores in Baxter County and now that she thought about it, a third collage was still sitting in the back of her closet, unsold, so that left only one unaccounted for. It had gone to a woman from right there in Serenity. That address was the closest so she'd go there before driving to Mountain Home and buying back her own pictures.

She had to reclaim all the keys. It was the only way to be sure she had the right ones. She shuddered. Her stomach clenched. Failing to please a man like her husband was unthinkable.

The trembling fingers of one hand clasped the receipts while she gently touched her cheek with the other, remembering previous encounters. She dared not fail.

ONE

Charlene Nancy Boyd, Chancy for short, loved antiques so much that she was willing to work 24/7 to find and preserve them. On balmy spring days like this one, however, she was happy to find a good excuse to leave her shop and venture into the beautiful Ozark hills. Dogwood trees had started to lose their white blossoms and the oaks were producing tiny chartreuse leaves that would grow, darken and soon fill the skyline.

The auction at the old farm place off Hawkins Mill Road was the kind that always made her sad. A couple's lifetime worth of belongings was being liquidated. Both Jewel and Pete Hawkins had passed away and their heirs were selling their entire estate, one piece at a time.

Those items that didn't interest surviving relatives were often the most valuable, Chancy knew, and she wanted to be there to bid. If she bought something that eventually brought a profit, fine. If she let nostalgia or enthusiasm influence her and paid too much, that was simply part of the business. She much preferred auctions to private sales because she was far too softhearted when it came to the old people who were selling their last treasures.

The crowd massing around the long tables of household goods set up in the farmyard was filled with familiar faces. Chancy greeted several acquaintances before she noticed Miss Mercy Cosgrove, a former schoolteacher she saw often, particularly in church.

Chancy waved and joined the elderly woman. "Morning. Great to see you. How've you been?"

The thin octogenarian gave her a welcoming hug, then shrugged. "Passable, considering. If I'd known how many aches and pains I'd have at this age I'd have taken better care of myself years ago."

"I know what you mean." The back of her hand rested against her lower back. She made a fist and rubbed a sore spot through her blue sweatshirt. "I get a catch every once in a while, too."

"Young thing like you?"

"I'm nearly thirty, Miss Mercy."

"That's impossible." She held out her hand waist-high. "I remember when you were only this tall. Cute little thing you were, too, not that you're not still pretty." Eyes misty with fond memories, she studied

Chancy's face. "Still got those adorable little dimples, I see. I imagine you have to beat the boys off with a stick."

Chancy couldn't help chuckling. In her teens she'd adjusted to the fact she wasn't popular the way many of the other girls were. "I think I may have hit a few of those guys too hard," she said with a smile. "Word must have gotten around because I haven't had to beat any of them off since high school." *And not really then, either.*

"Well, more's the pity," her former teacher said. She tittered behind her hand. "'Course, I shouldn't talk since I never remarried after my husband passed away."

"We're probably both smart to stay single," Chancy offered. "Marriage is highly overrated."

Mercy laid a hand on Chancy's arm. "Now, dear, you can't judge every couple by you know who."

She certainly did. The turbulence of her parents' union was well known to practically everybody, thanks to the longevity of juicy gossip in a small town. The atmosphere in the modest house where Chancy had grown up had been so volatile she'd moved out as soon as she'd been able to amass enough capital to start her business, and although that move had undoubtedly saved her life, she'd often wondered if her presence could have prevented her parents' untimely demise.

"I should have been there to talk some sense into them," Chancy said, remembering.

"Nonsense. Nobody can predict what a tornado's going to do. If they'd gone to the storm cellar like reasonable folks would have, they'd probably have survived. They were grown-ups, Chancy, honey. They made their choice and it was the wrong one. That's not your fault."

"I know, but…"

Mercy held up a hand. "Hush. No more of that silliness. You and I can no more be responsible for life and death than we can fly. When the good Lord decides my time is up and takes me home, I don't want anybody down here to blame themselves. I'm sure your mama and daddy don't, either." She smiled sweetly.

Chancy gave her a cautious hug, mindful of her frailty. "Thanks for reminding me who's really in charge, Miss Mercy. You always were a wise lady."

"Just repeating what the Good Book says."

In the background, the auctioneer began making his opening announcements. Chancy tensed, half listening while she asked, "Are you going to stay for the fun?"

"I wouldn't miss it. Got my eye on that green Depression-glass butter dish of Jewel's over there. Hope it doesn't go too high."

"I promise not to bid against you," Chancy said.

Her glance passed over the crowd, assessing the competition. She knew most of the antique dealers present and would try to pass the word to them to back off and let Miss Mercy have the winning bid for the butter dish. Most would listen. These were country people. They basically looked out for each other in a manner few outsiders could comprehend.

Interceding in this small way would be Chancy's opportunity to repay the former teacher who had befriended her as a child and provided a temporary refuge from the daily emotional storms she'd faced at home.

The remembrance of her unhappy childhood settled like a rock in her stomach. She consciously pushed aside the negative feelings and began to wend her way into the throng, intent on trying to influence the bidding in favor of her old friend and mentor. As far as she could tell, there were only three dealers present who consistently bought Depression glass. She'd start with them.

The twin-engine Cessna 310 flew low over Serenity and set up for a landing at the rural airstrip. There was no control tower but that didn't bother pilot, Nate Collins. Considering some of the storms he'd encountered in the course of his job, nothing much rattled him. The excitement of being a storm-chasing meteorologist had influenced him so deeply that he often felt a letdown when nothing dangerous was in the offing.

He banked, flared and set the wheels of the plane

on the numbers painted at the end of the short runway. The challenge of perfect wheel placement gave him gratification even though he could have safely landed much farther down the asphalt. Cutting the power, he taxied to transient parking where a beat-up old green pickup truck waited.

An elderly man wearing denim overalls and a frayed jacket over a blue shirt got out of the truck, shaded his eyes beneath the bill of a sweat-stained baseball cap and waved.

Nate set his jaw as he returned the greeting. Grandpa Ted looked more unsteady every time Nate visited. Good thing he'd done his homework and lined up a retirement home for him and Grandma Hester before he'd left Oklahoma. It was high time they gave up this hard, dreary lifestyle and moved into a place where they'd be properly taken care of. And where he could look in on them every day if need be, Nate added, feeling pleased with himself for having taken the initiative and solving everyone's problems ahead of time.

He turned off the plane's engines, secured the controls and climbed down to chock the wheels and tie the wings down. As soon as he'd finished, Ted greeted him with a bear hug and a slap on the shoulder while the old, shaggy, black-and-white farm dog riding in the back of the truck barked a greeting.

"Good to see ya, son," Ted said. "Good flight?"

"No problems," Nate answered, grabbing his overnight bag and laptop computer. "I see you've still got that noisy old dog."

"Yup. Domino and I are a pair. We're both still hangin' in there. He's good company, especially when I want to sit on the porch and watch the world go by."

"How've you been? And how's Grandma?"

"Oh, you know us," Ted said with a wide grin splitting his leathered face. "Even old age can't keep us down. Your Grandma's been bakin' ever since we heard you was comin'. She's made all your favorites."

Nate rubbed his flat stomach with his free hand. "Good thing I don't get to visit that often or I'd be fat as one of those pigs you used to raise when I was a kid."

"Speaking of being busy, how's the storm chasin' business? After all those hurricanes a few years back, are tornadoes startin' to look tame?"

Nate laughed and clapped the old man lightly on the back. "Not from where I stand. I'm glad I could sneak away for a few days. Tornado season is almost here and I never know what may pop up."

"How's this week look? Can you stick around a little while, do you think?"

"Probably. There's a high-pressure ridge in place that should keep most of the bad weather out of the plains, at least for a few days. I'll keep my eye on it."

Nate walked toward the truck with his grandfather

and paused to ruffle the old dog's silky ears before he asked Ted, "Mind if I drive? I still have a soft spot in my heart for this old pickup."

"Not at all. Keys are in it. It'll be my pleasure to just ride for a change." He chuckled as he hoisted the legs of his overalls and climbed stiffly into the passenger's seat. The door slammed with a rattle and a dull bang. "Reminds me of the time I was teachin' you to drive and you ran us into that ditch over by the Mullins place."

"In this very same truck, back when it was almost new. I'm amazed you didn't yell at me," Nate added. "We did have some good times, didn't we?"

"That, we did." Ted's shoulders shook with silent humor. "I wasn't too sure it was gonna work out when you first came to stay with us but you turned out all right, son. Yes, sir, you surely did."

"Thanks to you and Grandma Hester," Nate said, sobering. His fingers tightened around the steering wheel. "I owe you both a lot."

"Nonsense," Ted said. "You don't owe us a bloomin' thing, boy."

"Still, I'm thankful I'm in a position to take care of you the way you took care of me."

Watching his grandfather out of the corner of his eye to gauge his reaction, Nate saw him stiffen and push himself up straighter in the seat.

"You ain't gonna start that nonsense again, are you?"

Nate ignored his scowl. "It's not nonsense. You and Grandma deserve a chance to kick back and relax."

The old man sighed and shook his head as if he thought Nate was addled. "If I don't have my chores and my shop and Hester don't have her kitchen and garden to tend, we might as well curl up and die right now. I appreciate your concern, truly I do, but we're not ready to retire from life."

"Okay," Nate said. He didn't want to start off on a sour note. There'd be plenty of time to discuss making sensible changes during the remainder of his visit.

He drove out of the airport and headed down Byron Road. To his surprise, cars were parked on the grassy shoulder on both sides of the two-lane road as he neared its junction with Hawkins Mill Road.

"What's going on here?" Nate asked.

"Farm auction." Ted grimaced as if it pained him to say the words. "The Hawkins place. Jewel went first. Ol' Pete was lost without her. He didn't last three months after she died. Didn't think he would."

Nate arched an eyebrow but held his peace. Jewel and Pete Hawkins had been friends and neighbors of his grandparents for literally decades. Losing them both so close together had to have been difficult. He saw no need to point out the obvious correlation between their lives.

He slowed the truck, barely finding room to squeeze it through the single lane remaining between the parked vehicles, while Domino panted and paced from side to side in the truck bed, trying to sniff every vehicle they passed.

"Half the population of Fulton County must be here," Nate remarked with disdain. "Who taught these people how to park, anyhow?"

"Old geezers like me," Ted answered. "Your grandma wanted to come to the auction today but I talked her out of it. We'll never live long enough to wear out all the junk we've already got, let alone find good use for any of this stuff." When Nate's head snapped around, the elderly man guffawed. "That don't mean we're ready to pack it up and move to some fancy old folks' home, so don't go gettin' any funny ideas, y'hear?"

"Yes, sir."

Nate slowed even more, edging forward inches at a time rather than scrape one or more of the unevenly parked vehicles. "I don't believe these people. Don't they care about their cars?"

"Sure they do. They're just not in an all-fired hurry the way you are. Slow down. We're almost home. Those chocolate-chip cookies you're cravin' will wait."

Before Nate could comment, a slightly built woman staggered onto the roadway directly in front of him. She was carrying such a big box, her face was obscured and she obviously couldn't see where she was going. He slammed on the brakes to keep from hitting her, jammed the truck into neutral and jumped out, fully intending the deliver a lecture on safety that would turn her ears red.

The woman must have heard him screech to a halt and get out because she peeked around the side of the cardboard box and gave him a sheepish grin. "Sorry about that. I should have looked before I crossed. That's my van right over there. The tan one that says Chancy's Second Chances on the side. It's not locked. Do you mind?" She passed the bulky box to Nate with a smile. "Thanks. That was getting heavy."

Flabbergasted, he stood there in the middle of the road holding the box and staring after her as she turned and hurried back the way she'd come.

Traffic was beginning to pile up in both directions. Someone honked. Nate's head swiveled from side to side as if he were watching a professional tennis match. True to her word, the woman had vanished back into the rapidly dispersing auction crowd. Southern manners dictated that he deliver the box to her van whether he liked it or not, and given the worsening traffic jam, the sooner the better.

As he stepped out of the way, he noted that Ted had slid behind the wheel of the farm truck. The old man leaned out the open window to call, "Can't park here. I'll go turn around and come back for you."

Nate shook his head. "There's no need for that. Just get out of this mess and go on home. I'll walk over."

"You sure?"

"Positive. It's not far."

"Okay. I'll meet you at the house. Take your time."

"Yeah, right." Nate was miffed. Free time was the one thing he had far too little of. He'd come to Serenity for the sole purpose of convincing his grandparents to sell their small farm and move to Oklahoma where he could better look after them. He had *not* flown all those miles to waste one minute carrying useless junk to some peddler's wagon. He was a man on a mission, a man with an important goal.

Reaching the back door to the van, he rested the leading edge of the box against its bumper while he tried the handle. It didn't turn. It didn't even jiggle.

Nate was considering abandoning the enormous box when its owner returned.

"Sorry," she said pleasantly, "I forgot to mention that that door sticks. You have to give it a nudge to get it to open. Here. I'll do it."

There wasn't enough room between the parked vehicles for Nate to step back, let alone turn and put down the box. Consequently, he found himself leaning awkwardly with the backs of his legs pressed against the bumper and grille of the truck next in line, while the woman wedged herself in front of him and the box to fiddle with the van door.

She was a little older than she'd seemed at first glance, he decided, probably nearly his age, although with her sun-streaked, golden hair pulled back in a ponytail and no makeup, it was difficult to tell. One thing was certain, she wasn't afraid of hard work. It looked as though there was already enough heavy furniture crammed into her van to give anyone a good workout, let alone a woman her size.

She turned and tried to relieve him of the box. "Okay. I'll take that now."

Nate's ingrained chivalry had kicked in. "No problem. I've got it. Where shall I put it?"

Her laugh was light and full of cheerful self-deprecation. "Beats me. I think I may have over-bought."

"I have to agree with you there. I take it you have a business?"

"Yes." She pushed up the arms of her sweatshirt and extended her right hand. "I'm Chancy Boyd. Chancy's Second Chances is my antique store. Maybe you've seen it. I'm one block off the square, behind the grocery market."

"Sorry, no," Nate said. "I'm just visiting." He managed to shake her hand by shifting the box and temporarily supporting it with his forearm. "Nate Collins. My grandparents live right down the road."

"Hester and Ted? You're a Collins? Nice to meet you! Your grandparents are dears. No wonder you're being so helpful. It must run in the family."

Nate's guilty conscience kicked him in the gut. Had he lived in a bustling city so long that he'd forgotten his upbringing? Apparently so.

He hoisted the cardboard box aloft and managed to wedge it into the cargo space above a carved dresser. "Actually," he said as he brushed off his hands and the front of his lightweight jacket, "I got out of Ted's truck to yell at you for walking in front of me. You might have been run over."

Her bluish hazel eyes twinkled above a mischievous grin. "In that case, thanks for not smashing me flat."

"You're welcome." Nate was rapidly losing his annoyance in the face of this young woman's upbeat attitude. "So, how much more do you have to load?"

"You don't want to know." She made a face. "I'm sure I'll have to make two trips to the shop to carry it all. They started bunching little items in piles to get rid of everything at the end and I wound up with a lot more than I intended to buy."

She scanned the roadside. "You know, if we used your pickup truck to carry the excess we'd be done in no time. Where did you park it?"

"I didn't. I told Ted to take it and go on home."

"Bummer." Her forehead wrinkled with obvious

thought. "Say, since I've already settled my bill with the auctioneer, why don't we drive over to their house to see if Ted minds if we borrow it? What do you think?"

Nate raised an eyebrow. He had no intention of telling her what he was actually thinking because it was anything but complimentary. He knew that helping a neighbor was customary in these parts but that didn't mean he was ready to drop everything and come to her aid, even if her smile and dimples were pretty persuasive.

"Aren't you afraid to go off and leave your stuff unattended?" he asked.

Chancy pulled a face. "I suppose you do have a good point, even in a place like Serenity. But borrowing the truck would be faster than my going back to the shop and unloading enough stuff to make room for the rest in the van."

"Okay." Nate saw no graceful way to turn her down without sounding snobbish. He cleared off the van's passenger seat by gathering up a stack of framed photos and climbed in. "Then let's go. I'll just hold these while you drive. We can be back in a jiffy."

"Right. Thanks!" She got behind the wheel, fired up the motor and cautiously pulled into traffic.

Habit made Nate glance in the rearview mirror on his side. The crowd was breaking up and other vehicles were also trying to join the outflow. Several car lengths back a thin, weary-looking woman wearing a bandanna around her long, dark hair darted into the middle of the street and stopped to stare after them.

Nate saw a car bearing down behind her. His breath caught. As he watched, she apparently came to her senses, whirled and stepped out of the way at the last instant.

"I don't believe it," he muttered.

"What's the matter?"

"Nothing, now. I almost saw an accident. Don't you people ever look when you cross the street?"

Chancy laughed. "You're definitely not from around here, are you?"

"How'd you guess?"

"It was easy. Didn't you visit your grandparents when you were a boy?"

Nate sobered. "As a matter of fact, I lived with them for close to a year when I was finishing high school."

He saw her brow knit. Then, her eyes widened and she stared over at him. "Nate? You're Nasty Nathaniel? I don't believe it!"

He huffed. "It's been a long time since I've been called that. How nice of you to remember."

"Hey, I'm sorry. It's just that all the girls my age used to have terrible crushes on you. I think our par-

ents gave you that nickname to scare us, which had
the opposite effect, of course. You disappeared when
I was in the eighth grade. What happened?"

"I joined the Marines and then went on to college
and got my degree in meteorology. That's—"

"I know. You're a weatherman." She laughed
softly. "I suppose you thought I'd say you studied
meteors. Does that happen often?"

"All the time."

"Then it's my pleasure to prove we're not all
country-bumpkins around here, even if we don't always look both ways before crossing the street."

TWO

Chancy pulled up the winding, dusty drive and stopped her van in front of the two-story Collins farmhouse. It was a relic of a bygone era with the same kind of charm as the quaint antiques that filled her shop.

Hester had planted tall, colorful hollyhocks along a southwest-facing wall. The pale pink peonies were almost ready to flower and clematis vines had begun to creep up the archway framing the access to the front door. Soon after the peonies were done, an enormous hydrangea bush next to the raised porch would begin to droop under the weight of mop-head flowers in varying shades of pink and lavender. The overall effect was charmingly reminiscent of picture postcards prevalent in the forties and fifties.

Before Nate was fully out of the van his grandmother came dashing off the porch with a screech of delight and gathered him up in an ample welcoming hug. "I'm so proud you're here!"

Blushing, he nevertheless returned her affection-ate embrace. "I'm happy to see you, too."

"Well, come in, come in." She smiled at Chancy. "You, too, girl. Get out and come on in. You're al-ways welcome."

"Thanks, Miss Hester. But right now I've got more stuff to pick up from the auction. Nate said we might be able to borrow your farm truck to haul it, if you don't mind."

The old woman's gray eyebrows arched above the frames of her glasses and her smile widened as she looked from Chancy to Nate and back again. "'Course not. You two just go right ahead and take the truck. I'm glad to hear that some of poor Jewel's precious things found a good home. Ted didn't want me to go to the sale and I suppose he was right, I just wish…"

Breaking off, she glanced at the porch where her husband lounged in a white-painted rocking chair with the shaggy, black-and-white dog lying at his feet.

"If there's anything in the van you fancy I'll be glad to save it for you," Chancy offered.

"I know it's foolishness to value earthly posses-sions. Still…" Hester stood on tiptoe to peer in at the collection Chancy had amassed. "If I had just one special thing to remember Jewel by, it would do this old heart good."

Nate spoke up. "We really should be getting back

to the auction. Chancy left a big pile of stuff and we don't want it to walk off while she's gone."

"'Course you don't." Hester backed away from the van. "You go on, now. I don't need nothin'."

Nate had replaced the short stack of framed pictures and photos on the passenger seat when he'd gotten out. Chancy leaned over, gathered them up and passed them to Hester through the open window. "Here. Look through these and keep all you want. I know there are several nice pictures of Pete and Jewel in the pile. I just bought them for the old frames."

"Bless your sweet little heart," Hester said with tears in her eyes. "What do I owe you?"

"Not a thing," Chancy replied. "It's my pleasure."

"Then you have to come back for supper tonight. I fixed Nate's favorite. Pot roast. We'll eat as soon as y'all are done haulin' and unloadin'."

The look she shot her flabbergasted grandson allowed no argument so he immediately swallowed his objections and formally backed her up. "Yes. Please join us. I know you must be too tired to go home and cook."

"That's the truth," Chancy said. "All right. I'll be happy to come for supper. Thanks for asking."

As Nate turned and headed for the pickup truck, he was shaking his head. Somehow, his well-thought-out plans for a serious talk with his grandparents had been sidetracked big-time. Well, it couldn't be helped now. All he could hope for at this point was a peaceful meal and not too much inane conversation.

He snorted in self-deprecation. Anybody who recalled his detested nickname from a good fifteen years ago was probably full of colorful remembrances about his escapades as a wild teen; events he hoped his grandparents had either forgiven or forgotten. Or both.

The first thing he was going to have to do was win over Chancy Boyd and ask her not to make any embarrassing references to his past. The best way to ensure that, he reasoned, was to help her haul her auction purchases in Ted's truck and then also offer to unload them.

It wasn't a task Nate particularly relished volunteering for but in his view, some serious PR work was called for.

The auction was over and traffic had thinned by the time Chancy and Nate arrived back at the Hawkins place so they were easily able to find parking places. She drove past the closest one and left it for him so they could more efficiently load the truck.

Gesturing and pointing as she walked back toward him she called, "Over there. By that lilac bush. That whole pile is mine."

"Wow. When you shop you don't kid around, do you?"

Chancy had to chuckle at his astounded expression in spite of the fact she felt the same way when she looked at the enormous stack of bags and boxes. "Nope. When they group items like they did, it's almost more trouble than it's worth. Still, every once in a while I discover I've bought something really rare or valuable that I didn't even know was there."

"I hardly know where to start picking this up."

"I know what you mean." Pausing, hands fisted on her hips, Chancy scowled as she perused the haphazard pile of merchandise.

"What's the matter?" Nate asked.

"I don't know. It looks kind of messy, like somebody stirred it."

"How in the world would you know?"

"I suppose you're right. It just seems worse than it was when I put it here." She shrugged. "Oh, well. Just grab any old box and let's start stacking them in your truck. I don't think there's anything breakable. All the glass and china is already in my van."

"Gotcha." He grinned at her. "I mean, yes, ma'am."

"You can drop the fake Southern charm," Chancy said, mirroring his amiable expression. "Just keep up the Southern gentleman act for a while longer and I'll be satisfied."

Nate passed her carrying a precarious-looking stack of tattered cardboard boxes. "What makes you think it's an act? Maybe I'm a true Southern gentleman. After all, Ted's my granddad and you already said you liked him."

Laughing lightly, she gathered up an armload of old blankets and quilts and followed Nate. "That's true. And kinship is very important around here."

After she'd unceremoniously crammed the blankets into the pickup bed, they started back to the main pile together. "Lots of young people leave the Ozarks, thinking things must be better in faraway places, then find out otherwise and come home again," Chancy observed. "Is that what your parents did?"

"No. Dad never wanted to come back here to live. My mother was city born and bred. She viewed life on the farm as one step out of the Stone Age. Never would even agree to visit after the first time."

"That's too bad. No wonder you didn't fit in very well when you came to stay with Ted and Hester."

"I've been meaning to talk to you about that," Nate said seriously as they continued to work. "I'd appreciate it if you didn't mention any of the trouble I had when I was here before."

"Why not? I remember thinking that the local boys were treating you terribly. If it had been me, I'd have gotten mad and socked a few of them in the nose long before you did."

"Just the same. Please?"

"Sure." Chancy shrugged as she scooped up several

paper grocery sacks containing odd bits of fabric and yarn. "No problem. I won't breathe a word."

"Thanks."

"You're welcome. Just stick the rest of that stuff in the truck. I'll go put these bags in the front of the van so the little pieces don't blow all over town and then you can follow me to the shop. Okay?"

"Sure. One more trip and I'll have it all."

"Good. I…" Her jaw dropped. Thunderstruck, she blinked and scanned the street as if positive she'd simply made a mistake. Unfortunately, there was no mistake. "I don't believe it!"

Nate paused beside her with the last of the boxes. "What? What's wrong?"

"My van," Chancy said breathlessly. "It's gone."

"What are you talking about? It can't be gone. We were right here the whole time."

"I wasn't watching it, were you?"

"Well, no, but…" He scowled at her. "You didn't leave the keys in it, did you?"

"Of course I did. I always do. My logo is all over the side. Who in his right mind would take a vehicle so easy to identify?"

"Obviously somebody who didn't think that far ahead." Nate reached into his jacket pocket, pulled out a cell phone and tried to hand it to her. "Here. Call the police."

Chancy snorted derisively. "Right now, I think there

are two sheriff's cars in the whole county and only one deputy besides the sheriff, himself. What makes you think reporting the theft would do any good?"

"Okay. Then, what do you suggest?"

"We chase them."

"Chase them? How? We don't have any idea which way they went."

"Well, it's better than just standing here staring at each other while my van gets farther and farther away, isn't it?"

Nate sighed heavily. "Get in the truck." He grabbed the bags from her arms and tossed them into the bed with the other auction purchases. "Like you said, it'll be easy to ID your van, assuming we can catch up to it."

Chancy didn't see any better options. If whoever had taken her van intended to sell its contents, there would be no way to prove ownership once all that furniture was dispersed. And if the van itself was the target of the theft it could be repainted and sold or parted out. She needed her van for work. Desperately. Without it, she might as well quit the antique business.

Piling into the front seat of the pickup beside Nate, she slammed the door. "Okay, I'm in. Floor it."

Chancy didn't know how much stuff was blowing or bouncing out of the bed of the truck as they careened around corners and bumped through potholes but she didn't care. They could always backtrack and clean up any mess later. Right now, she had other goals.

Nate skidded to a halt at the stop sign by the post office, where Byron Road intersected with Highway 62. Chancy had to brace herself against the dusty dashboard to stay on the seat.

"Which way?" he asked.

"I don't know. Just drive."

"That's stupid. We won't accomplish a thing if we wrap this truck around a tree. You live here. Think. Where would you go if you wanted to hide a van with a big logo on it?"

"Are you kidding? There are dozens of dirt roads all over this county. Any one of them would do." She held out her hand. "Give me your phone?"

He handed it over without argument. "Are you finally going to be sensible and call the sheriff?"

"Yes, and no," she said. "The first thing I'm going to do is start the prayer chain from my Sunday-school class."

"What good will *that* do?"

Chancy huffed. "Plenty. Besides the value of prayer itself, it'll give us lots more eyes all over town. Nothing gets past those women. They all know me. If my van is near any of their houses, we'll hear about it."

"Ah, the small-town spy network. Why didn't I think of that?"

She couldn't resist making a joke in spite of the trying situation. "Because you're not from around here." The way Nate's dark eyebrows arched over his narrowed brown eyes almost made her laugh.

Only one phone number came to mind immediately so Chancy dialed it, hoping desperately that her friend was at home. It rang twice before she heard a cheery "Hello."

"Louella!" *Thank You, God.* "This is Chancy. My van's been stolen and I want you to pass the word to everybody as fast as you can."

"Where are you? What happened?" the other woman asked.

"It's a long story. I was at the Hawkins auction and somebody drove off with all my stuff. Tell everybody I can be reached at…" She covered the mouthpiece and turned to Nate. "What's the number of this phone?" He told her and she repeated it to Louella.

"That's not your regular number is it?"

"No." Chancy made a face and glanced sideways at Nate, knowing what he'd think and wishing she didn't have to explain when he could overhear. "My purse was in the van with my keys. I've lost my phone, my wallet, my checkbook, everything."

"Oh, you poor thing. I'll telephone the girls right away. Want me to call the sheriff, too?"

"Yes, please," Chancy said. "I'll be at the number I gave you. Please hurry."

Nate waited till she'd hung up before he commented. "You really are amazing."

"Why? Because I'm dumb enough to let some lowlife drive off with my whole life?"

"No, because you're trusting enough to leave things sitting around in the first place. My grandparents refuse to listen to me and lock their doors at night, but that's not nearly as bad as leaving keys in an ignition."

"The keys were in this truck when we borrowed it," she reminded him. "You have to understand how safe it normally is in a place like Serenity. We don't have a lot of crime here. It's like living in a bygone era."

"Even the Old West had crime," Nate countered.

"True. I guess I just figured the good Lord would look after my stuff." She could tell by his expression that he thought she was seriously deluded.

"I should have known," he said. "Didn't it ever occur to you that your God-given brain was meant to be used for something besides a place to grow hair?"

"I've never heard it put quite like that but, yes, I guess I do bear some of the responsibility."

"Some of it? You bear *all* of it."

She flinched. "I wouldn't go that far."

It didn't surprise her much when he replied, "Well, I sure would."

Nate felt as helpless as a feather caught in one of the tornadoes he was so fond of chasing. They had covered most of the town and were working in widening circles to survey the outlying countryside. It had occurred to him earlier that they were on a wild goose chase but he kept hoping they'd spot Chancy's missing van just the same.

Finally, he pulled over and stopped on the unpaved shoulder of the road. "Look. I'm sorry. This isn't doing any good and we both know it." It bothered him to see her shoulders slump with such dejection.

She sighed noisily. "I suppose you're right. What time is it, anyway?"

"Nearly seven." Looking at his watch he remembered their promise to his grandparents. "Uh-oh. I think we'd better call Grandma and tell her what's going on. She's probably still waiting on us for supper."

"Oh, no. Poor Hester. I'm so sorry. I wasn't thinking about anything but myself."

"She'll understand." Nate pulled out the phone and pushed the button to speed dial.

"It's me," he said when Ted answered. "Chancy and I got hung up. We're sorry if we put you out. Her van was stolen and we've been driving around looking for it."

"Stolen?" The older man was incredulous.

"Yes, stolen. Right out from under our noses. One minute it was there and the next minute it was gone.

We have no idea who took it or why but we thought maybe we could spot it if we drove around for a while."

"Where did you see it last?" Ted asked.

"At the auction. Why?"

"Hold on. I thought I saw some activity over at the Hawkins place a few minutes ago. I'm gonna walk out on the porch for a second and take a closer look."

Nate scowled while he waited. Patience had never been one of his virtues and he hated being put on hold, even for the short time it would take his grand-father to accomplish whatever was on his mind.

Ted returned with a question. "Where are you?"

"Over on the highway near Hickory Station. Why?"

"Well, I suggest you hightail it back here. Every-body else is gone but it appears to me that light brown van of hers is sittin' smack-dab in front of the Hawkins place."

"It can't be."

Ted guffawed. "Oh, yeah? Sure looks like it. 'Course, I could be mistaken. It's a ways over there and it's gettin' dark so I can't see real clear. Still, it might pay you to come on back and have a look-see."

"Thanks. Keep your eye on it till we get there. We're on our way."

He glanced at the worried young woman sitting next to him and answered her unspoken question. "My granddad thinks he sees your van back at the

Hawkins place. I don't know how that can possibly be but he sounds pretty certain."

"Praise the Lord!" Chancy was clapping her hands and grinning from ear to ear. "The prayer chain worked again."

Nate huffed as he whipped the truck around and floored the accelerator. As far as he was concerned there had to be a sensible explanation for whatever had happened. Just because he couldn't see the details of it didn't mean he was ready to resort to giving credit to prayer or anything else unseen. It was far more likely that kids had taken the van joyriding, had had an attack of conscience and had decided to bring it back before they got in trouble with the law. It was just the kind of adolescent folly that had gotten him into trouble as a teen.

He considered expressing his opinion on the matter then decided against it. Although he did concede the probability of a Creator, he wasn't willing to believe that God cared about the minute details of everyday life on earth.

He caught her peering at him. "What?"

"You don't believe in prayer, do you?"

"Maybe. Maybe not."

"Wow." She settled back against the seat and stared out the window at the passing scenery for a while before she said, "I'm sorry. I didn't mean to make you uncomfortable."

"No problem. You're entitled to your beliefs."

"And you're entitled to yours. I guess I've just lived in the Bible Belt for so long I forgot there were folks who didn't think the same way I do." She paused. "What brought you back to Serenity, anyway? Are you just visiting?"

"Not exactly," Nate said. It seemed the perfect opportunity to draw her into his confidence and enlist her aid so he said, "I came to talk some sense into my grandparents. I want them to move to Oklahoma."

Her eyes widened. "Whatever for?"

"For their own good," Nate said flatly. "I have the perfect place already picked out between Oklahoma City and Norman, where I work. They'll have everything money can buy and they won't have to lift a finger. They'll love it. And I'll be close enough to look in on them more often."

He noted that Chancy was staring at him as if he'd suddenly grown two heads or sprouted horns, so he said, "I take it you disagree?"

"Oh, yeah," she drawled. "That's a real understatement."

"I don't see why."

"Because it's the stupidest thing I've ever heard, that's why."

Nate couldn't help giving her a lopsided smile. "Hey, don't hold back," he taunted. "Tell me what you really think."

THREE

The dark-haired young woman hiding behind the tangle of wild honeysuckle vines along Hawkins Mill Road watched Chancy reclaim her van and drive away.

She'd missed bidding on the collage with the keys because the stupid auctioneer hadn't recognized its value. When he'd bunched it with all those other pictures from the Hawkins estate, the crowd had pressed so close she hadn't seen that it was included in that lot until it was too late.

She sighed and blinked back tears. Well, at least she knew where her picture had gone and who had it. That was something. She would have approached the buyer and offered to purchase the small collage right away if she hadn't been afraid of calling undue attention to it. Now, she wished she had marshaled her courage and done so.

What she couldn't understand was why she hadn't been able to locate it in the pile of goods the buyer had left behind or later, in the van. It had to be there somewhere. She'd seen the woman carry it off amid all her other purchases, but then she'd lost track of it.

"I was just too frantic," she reasoned. "I didn't take long enough to look through all those things properly. I shouldn't have gotten scared and returned the van till I was positive." Well, it was too late now. Her hands were trembling and she felt sick to her stomach even though she hadn't remembered to eat that day.

"What now? What would Sam do?" she wondered aloud.

A shiver of remembrance skittered up her spine and made the fine hairs at the back of her neck prickle. A better question was what would Sam do to her in a couple of weeks when he got out of prison? If she didn't get her hands on all the keys she'd so recklessly lost, she knew she'd be in terrible trouble.

Her dusty blue sedan was parked in the driveway of an abandoned house just down the road. Since there was nothing more she could do with regard to searching Chancy's van or antique shop today, she was going to get in her car and head for Mountain Home to buy back the other two collages.

"Please, God, let them be there," she prayed under her breath. If those pictures, too, had been passed to new owners she didn't know what she was going to do.

Tears of frustration threatened again. She fought them back. Who did she think she was, calling on

God for anything? Her whole life had been one sin after another so why would He care what happened to her? She should be thankful no one had caught her driving that van and had her arrested. Instead, she was asking for more favors. What a fool she was.

Alone now, she climbed out of the overgrown ditch and onto the roadbed where she could dust off the legs of her jeans. It was a little early in the season for chiggers but chances were she'd picked up dozens of ticks or other insect bites by hiding in the brush. Well, that couldn't be helped. A few itchy places were a small price to pay for having gotten away with car theft.

She smiled slightly. Maybe, when Sam came home and she told him about her escapade, he'd actually be proud of her.

"Not unless I get all his keys back," she countered. That was enough to spur her into a trot. The sooner she drove to Mountain Home and picked up those other pictures, the sooner she could be back in Serenity and resume her search there.

Ted and his old dog came off the porch together to greet Nate and Chancy when they drove in and parked their respective vehicles.

"I see it *was* her van," Ted said. "I watched you pick it up."

Nate pulled the keys from the ignition and handed

the ring to his grandfather. "Yes. And I suggest you not leave your keys in the truck anymore. It's too chancy."

She joined them with a slightly embarrassed grin. "Was that a pun?"

"What?" His brow knit. "Oh. No. Sorry. I didn't think about that being your name. It was just good advice."

"In this case I'm afraid I have to agree," she said, sobering. "I don't know what this world is coming to. We never used to have to worry about anything like that in Serenity."

"Wrong," Nate replied. "You always needed to, you just refused to see things clearly until today when you were forced to. Overlooking crime won't make it go away, it just makes you a more likely victim."

"Cynic."

"Realist is more like it."

Ted chuckled. "You two sound like Hester and me when we're arguing about something. Come on. She's nearly got supper on the table. We'd best go in."

"I'm sorry to have made everything so late," Chancy said. "I can't imagine who had my van."

The old man's bushy gray eyebrows arched over twinkling eyes. "You know, if y'all were teenagers, I'd think you'd made up a tall tale so you could go joyridin' instead of come on home to eat."

"We didn't!" Chancy insisted.

Ted laughed again. "I know. I keep a pretty close

watch on the neighborhood and I didn't see that van over there till a few minutes before you called and I told you about it."

"Did you see who brought it back?" Nate asked.

"Nope. Sorry. But I do know for sure it wasn't sittin' there the whole afternoon." He looked to Chancy. "If you told the sheriff it was stolen you'd best tell him he can quit lookin' for it."

"That's right. I totally forgot!" She pulled a face and grimaced at Nate. "And that's not all I forgot. You're right about us being too complacent around here. I was so glad to get all my things back, including my purse and cell phone, I never thought about not touching the steering wheel or door handle to preserve fingerprints. I imagine the sheriff is going to be really upset with me."

"If the thief is a kid, as I suspect, it's probably just as well," Nate said. "I can remember a few times when I was glad the law in Serenity wasn't as thorough as a city department might be."

She eyed him incredulously and saw a light of recognition in his eyes. After asking her to keep quiet about his youthful escapades, he'd just intimated he'd been in trouble and had therefore done exactly what he'd warned her against! It was funny to see a guy who was now so straight-laced struggle to think of a way to cover up his careless comment.

"Well," she drawled in his defense, "boys will be

boys. Since there was no harm done I guess it's just as well I messed up the fingerprints. I'm sure we've all done a few things we aren't proud of when we were growing up."

Ted laughed as he led the way into the farmhouse. "I have tipped a few outhouses in my time," he confessed. "But don't you dare tell Hester. Her pa was sittin' in one of 'em when I shoved it over. I thought it was her big brother in there. He'd threatened to beat me up if I kissed his sister and I was meanin' to get him back for it."

Chancy covered her mouth to muffle her giggles. "You didn't!"

"Yup. I surely did. Boy, was that old man mad. He came boilin' out of there ready for a fight. I hightailed it for the barn and hid till he went back in the house. Talk about scared. I was sure he'd find out and keep me from marryin' Hester, but if he knew the truth he never let on."

She started to follow Nate and his grandfather into the kitchen when she remembered she'd left her purse in her van. Again. If Nate realized what she'd done she'd be in for another of his lectures and that was not number one on the list of things she'd like to hear.

"You two go ahead," she said. "I'll be right with you. I just need to run back to the van for a second."

"Make yourself at home and come on in whenever you're ready," Ted said magnanimously.

Nate followed his grandfather into the kitchen and they both hung their jackets on pegs on the wall. Hester was at the stove, warming the food, and Nate gave her a quick kiss on the cheek as he peeked over her shoulder. "Mmm. Something smells good."

"I hope it's still fit to eat," she said. "What in the world's been goin' on, anyway?"

"It's a long story."

"Where's Chancy?"

"She went to get something out of her van. She'll be along in a sec."

"You be careful you don't say anything unkind to her or upset her, you hear? She's had it pretty rough these last few years."

"She has? Why?"

Lowering her voice, the older woman took him aside to explain, "Her folks were killed by that tornado that blew through here a couple of years ago. Remember it?"

"Sure. It mostly took the tops out of the trees. If I remember right, it was only an F-1 on the Fujita scale. I didn't realize Chancy's parents were involved."

"Well, they were. She took it pretty hard when she lost 'em both at once. She'd been on her own for a while before that but I think she blamed herself just the same."

"For an accident of nature? Why would she feel responsible?"

"Because she wasn't there to talk them into

taking cover, I reckon. Her ma and pa used to fight all the time and she'd do her best to calm 'em down. I wouldn't be surprised if those two hardheaded parents of hers were squabbling with their last breaths."

Nate nodded. "I see. Thanks for telling me. It'll keep me from putting my foot in my mouth."

In the background his grandfather cackled. "Oh, I wouldn't be so sure about that. You did a fair job of eatin' your shoe when you were talkin' out in the yard a few minutes ago."

Chancy grabbed her shoulder bag, used her cell phone to quickly explain to her friend Louella what had happened, then called the sheriff to end the stolen-vehicle search.

Slamming the van door, she glanced at her reflection in the dusty side mirror. Any lipstick she'd had on in the morning was long gone and the ever-present freckles on the bridge of her nose stood out like spots on a hound dog. She looked about sixteen and felt at least fifty, maybe older. What a day this had been!

Pausing to remove her dusty sweatshirt and smooth her hair, she tried to convince herself it didn't matter what she looked like. She was among friends, people who would accept her as she was. That was one of the things she liked best about living in a place like Serenity. Folks took each other at face value.

Then again, Nate Collins wasn't exactly a run-of-the-mill resident, was he? He was as handsome as any man pictured in magazine ads and twice as interesting; him with that dark, wavy hair and those coffee-brown eyes that seemed to see right into her. Too bad she didn't look at least as presentable as usual, wasn't it?

Disgusted that she'd even think about wanting to impress Nate, she stuck out her tongue at the image looking back at her from the small mirror. Who cared? Certainly not her. As a matter of fact, she was glad she was so plain and natural-looking. Hopefully, that would convince him she wasn't interested in him the way so many of her contemporaries had been when he'd lived here as a high-school senior.

In a way, Chancy felt as if she'd suddenly reverted to the awkward girl she'd been back then, particularly in the pit of her stomach. For some reason her long-banished teenage butterflies had reappeared and were creating a storm of flutters the likes of which she hadn't felt for years. That was silly, of course. She was far from being a child and had plenty of hard-earned maturity to call upon in a situation such as this.

She straightened, squared her shoulders, tugged the hem of her T-shirt over her jeans-clad hips and headed for the house. If she hadn't been worried about hurting Hester's and Ted's feelings she'd have climbed into her van and driven away. The notion was appealing. Then again, it wouldn't accomplish a thing in the long run. She still had to deal with Nate long enough to get her auction purchases unloaded from Ted's truck. Besides, everyone was waiting for her in the kitchen. The only gracious thing to do was swallow her pride and join them.

She patted the dog in passing, then entered the house and started across the small living room, following her nose toward the delicious smells coming from the country kitchen. In the few strides it took her to get there she laid aside her purse and reclaimed her confidence.

"Sorry if I kept y'all," she said brightly, concentrating on Hester. "Is there anything I can do to help?"

"Not a thing," the older woman said with a smile. "Table's set and everything's hotted up. Just grab a chair and let's eat."

Ted was already seated at the rectangular dining table at one end of the kitchen. Nate held a chair for Chancy then tried to do the same for his grandmother.

She shooed him away. "Nonsense. I got work to do. Y'all just sit down and let me take care of this."

Ted laughed. "Might as well mind her. When Hester gets a bee in her bonnet she's as stubborn as a mule."

Apparently amused by the mixed metaphor, Nate waited while she made two more trips to the table carrying a bowl of mashed potatoes and a dish of dark gravy with a ladle. Then, she settled into a chair next to her husband and Nate took the only remaining place, next to Chancy.

Chancy felt as if someone had plugged her finger into a fence charger. She knew if her hair hadn't been pulled back into a ponytail, it would be standing straight up. The fine curls at the nape of her neck certainly tickled enough!

She kept her eyes on the red-and-white checkered tablecloth as she carefully placed a paper napkin across her lap. Off to one side she saw a flash of movement. Nate had started to reach for his fork, then had stopped abruptly.

She blinked nervously and bowed her head as Ted began to say grace over the food. Obviously Nate wasn't used to praying before a meal and had nearly forgotten that his grandparents always said grace. How strange it must seem for him here. And how sad it was that he didn't really fit in, that he probably never had. No wonder he was so determined to get his family to leave Serenity.

Her personal unease forgotten, Chancy began to pray silently for him. *Lord, Nate has missed so much. Please show him how happy we are here and help him to understand, to share in what we've found.*

Those simple thoughts calmed her fears and replaced them with an amazing tenderness toward the man beside her. It wasn't she who needed to remember that she was acceptable just the way she was, it was Nate. For all his worldly polish and education, he was still needy, still on the outside looking in. Perhaps he always had been.

She would befriend him while he was here, she vowed. And maybe, just maybe, she could help him see why his grandparents were so content; why it was so very wrong to insist that they leave their perfect little home and move to unknown, unfamiliar territory.

Surely, given the facts, Nate would change his mind. After all, he was a thinking human being with the same God-given instincts they all shared. Just because he was a well-educated man didn't mean he wasn't approachable. Or did it?

FOUR

Supper progressed rapidly, due in part to the delay. Appetites were primed and even Chancy ate more than usual.

When Hester tried to press second helpings on her, however, she raised her hands, palms out, and politely demurred. "No, thanks. It was delicious but I couldn't eat another bite."

"Little thing like you?" Hester said. "You need to add a few more pounds or you're liable to blow away in a stiff breeze."

Chancy tried to hide her instinctive reaction to the innocent comment but she couldn't avoid comparing it to what had actually happened to her parents. Judging by the look of distress on Hester's face she, too, had realized exactly what she had said and the sudden silence at the table was noticeable.

Nate cleared his throat and provided a welcome distraction. "So, Chancy, do you want me to follow you to your shop so we can get your stuff unloaded tonight? I hate to leave it exposed in the bed of Grandpa's pickup all night. Never can tell when it might rain."

She couldn't help being amused. "You're the weatherman. Is that your professional opinion?"

"I haven't been studying recent reports but you know what they say about Arkansas weather. If you don't like it, wait a few minutes and it'll change."

"That's the truth." She rose from the table and reached for her plate. "Just let me help Hester clean up and we can head for my shop. It shouldn't take too long to move everything indoors."

The older woman immediately sprang to her feet and wrested the plate from Chancy's hands. "Nonsense. I always wash and Ted dries. We've been doing it that way for nearly fifty years and it's worked fine. Now, scat. We'll take care of straightening everything up."

Chancy hesitated. "Are you sure? I hate to leave you with a mess."

"Comes the day I can't do my own dishes, I'll give up cookin'," Hester replied. "Go on. Time's a wastin'."

Looking to Nate for guidance, Chancy asked, "Is she always this stubborn?"

His gaze rested tenderly on his grandmother. "No. Sometimes she's much worse. And when she makes up her mind there's no arguing with her, at least not right then." He leaned down to give Hester a parting peck on the cheek. "Don't work too hard. I'll be back with the truck as soon as I can."

"Take your time, children," the older woman replied.

Nate had ushered Chancy out onto the porch before she started to giggle. "Children?"

He chuckled, too. "I know. It is funny, isn't it? I suppose, no matter how old I get, I'll still be a kid in their eyes."

"How old are you, anyway?" Chancy asked.

"Mid-thirties. How about you?"

"Twenty-eight, going on eighty-two," she quipped, rubbing her back at the waist. "I shouldn't sit so still after a day of heavy lifting like today. I'm really starting to feel the muscle strain."

He walked her to her van, opened the door and held it for her. "We'll get you unloaded in no time. Then you can put your feet up and relax."

That made Chancy laugh again. "Relax? You obviously work for somebody else. People who run small businesses like mine don't have the luxury of taking time off."

"You can't work 24/7."

"Of course not." She tossed her purse in ahead of her and climbed into the van. "I go to church on Sundays."

Nate shut the door and backed away. "Right. Well, give me a minute to start the truck and I'll follow you."

As he turned and walked to the waiting pickup, Chancy watched him, pondering his reaction to her simple statement. Apparently, saying grace at the table was not the only practice of faith Nate Collins wasn't used to. Unless she missed her guess, he wasn't much for church attendance, either, which might help explain his off-putting reaction when she had given credit to God for answered prayer. She sighed. His closed-minded attitude probably bothered Hester and Ted a lot more than either of them let on.

Well, the night was young, she thought, starting the van and letting it idle while she watched Nate don his jacket before climbing into the cab of the truck. It wouldn't hurt him to humor his grandparents and attend church while he was in Serenity. And in case he hadn't thought of doing so for their sakes, she was going to look for an opportunity to suggest it.

Given the horrible losses she had experienced in the past few years, Chancy didn't know how she would have coped without her faith, weak as it was. How anyone got through life without knowing and trusting God was an unfathomable mystery to her, one she had long ago given up trying to solve. Maybe someday she'd understand why things had happened the way they had. Maybe she never would. That wasn't the real issue.

As far as her parents were concerned, she was the

one who had failed, not God. When she'd had a strong, unmistakable urge to go by their house and see them, she'd resisted because she hadn't wanted to listen to their squabbling. And they had died. It was as simple as that.

Logic and Bible teaching told her that God forgave her. What she couldn't seem to do was forgive herself.

Darkness had crept into the empty antique shop behind the grocery store as the sun had set. The prowler had not come prepared to stay so long.

She squinted, trying to see, as she sorted through stacks of merchandise that had yet to be priced and placed on the shelves in the front. Once the precious collage went on sale there was no telling who might buy it or how soon it would be sold. If it left Serenity, say in the hands of a tourist, it could end up anywhere.

The young woman brushed away tears of frustration. How could she have been so careless, so thoughtless? Why, oh why, hadn't she mustered enough gumption to offer to buy the collage when she'd realized she'd missed the bid at the auction? Maybe the dealer would have sold it to her. And maybe the antique buyer would have sensed the desperation in her offer and raised the price far beyond her ability to pay.

Well, there was no use speculating. It was too late

to do this the easy way. Now, she had to either locate the valuable artwork and steal it, or take the chance it might come up for sale soon without her knowledge.

She was not willing to wait and see. Time was running out.

Nate followed Chancy down Main to Church Street and through the pothole-riddled alleyway next to the small grocery market. The area appeared to be even more run-down than he'd remembered.

He brought the pickup to a stop behind the van, careful to leave plenty of room for unloading. By the time he climbed out and joined Chancy at the rear door of her shop, she was already fiddling with a ring of keys.

"That's odd," she muttered.

"What is?"

"This door. I could have sworn I left it locked."

"You didn't?"

"I guess not. When I went to turn the key, it was already open."

"Are you sure?"

"Relatively."

Even in the dimly lit alleyway he could see her sheepish smile so he said, "In other words, maybe not."

"Okay. Maybe not." Giving the knob a twist she swung the door open. "Wait here. I have to go into the front to turn on the lights."

"You don't have a switch back here?"

"No. I'm only renting and I never saw a need to rewire the place. It's a little inconvenient but I usually open the front first and take care of everything from there."

Nate peered into the crowded storeroom. "This place is a maze. How can you navigate in the dark without getting hurt?"

"Easy. I know where everything is."

"Still, I don't think you should try it. I'm sure there's a flashlight in the truck. Hold on. I'll go get it."

Chancy rolled her eyes as he jogged away. How silly he was being. She'd managed just fine all these years without anyone telling her what to do or how to do it, and she wasn't about to listen to the advice of some bossy city slicker, no matter how well intentioned he might be.

She swung open the heavy wooden door, stepped inside the barnlike storage area and gave her eyes a few moments to adjust to the lack of light.

Armless side chairs hung from the rafters by pegs and below them, armoires, dressers, desks and other heavy pieces of oak and mahogany furniture stood in rows like sentinels, guiding her path. Admittedly the way was narrow but as long as she stuck to the main aisle she knew she couldn't go astray. Besides, the longer she stood there the better she could see. Sort of.

Sliding one hand along the top of the nearest chest of drawers, she extended her other arm in front of her and started into the labyrinth that was her stockroom. She always kept the floor clear, so she knew there would be no unseen obstacles. She'd have the lights on and everything squared away long before Nate got back with his unnecessary flashlight.

Suddenly, there was a skittering, scraping sound to her right. Chancy froze. "Nate? Is that you?"

No one answered. The hair on the back of her neck stood on end. She held her breath. Listened. The only thing she could hear was the rapid beating of her own heart as it echoed in her ears.

Logic told her she was alone. Instinct told her otherwise. Logic suggested the presence of mice. Instinct insisted on a prowler, instead.

Well, there was no sense just standing there, she reasoned. If she backed out the door, she could reenter with Nate. If she pressed forward, she could turn on the light and banish her groundless fears. Relying on him did not appeal to her one bit. Proving her mettle, especially to him, sounded a lot more appealing.

Feeling her way ahead, Chancy continued toward the light switch. Just a few more steps. Just...

Her toe connected with a solid object where none should have been. Startled, she faltered, felt herself falling and flailed her arms to try to regain her balance.

It was no use. She hit the floor with a thud and

found herself draped partway across a cardboard box crammed with old frames and photographs. Glass tinkled with the impact. Pain shot up her arm from her hand.

Chancy shrieked.

"Where are you?!" Nate was shouting.

"Over here. On the floor."

The beam of a small flashlight swept quickly across the room and settled on her face, blinding her.

"What happened?" Nate demanded, hurrying toward her.

"I tripped." Holding out her hand, she blinked as she stared at her bleeding palm. "Uh-oh. I think I landed in some glass."

He crouched beside her. "Let me see."

"It's okay." Chancy pointed. "Get the lights, will you? The switch is on the other side of that doorway behind me."

"All right. Stay put so you don't cut yourself any worse. I'll be right back."

Chancy wasn't about to argue with him this time. Her hand throbbed and her knees didn't feel all that good, either, although she didn't think she'd cut anything but her palm. How could she have been so careless? Was she so scatterbrained that she'd left a box in the aisle and hadn't remembered doing it? Apparently.

Behind her, the beam from Nate's flashlight raked

across the wall. Its brightness made the rest of the storeroom seem even darker, the shadows deeper. The same skittering noise, now farther away, once again caught Chancy's attention.

Squinting, she peered into the gloom. Was that a human shape? Her breath caught and held. She strained to listen, to see.

"Nate! Hurry!" she called, scrambling to her feet. "Turn those lights on!"

As soon as he flipped the switch, the sinister form vanished.

Nate was beside her in a heartbeat. "What is it? What's wrong?"

"I—I thought I saw something—someone—over by the door." Chancy instinctively leaned closer to him.

"Wait here."

"No!" She grabbed his arm and held tight. "It's gone now." To her relief he remained with her, even slipping his arm lightly around her shoulders as soon as she released her hold.

"If you're sure."

"I am. The lights blinded me for a second. I guess I was imagining things." She glanced at the shards of glass and broken frames at her feet. "I can't believe I was so careless as to leave that right in the middle of the aisle."

"Maybe you didn't," Nate said.

"I must have."

"If you say so." His arm tightened around her. "You're shaking."

"Probably from shock," she said, holding her wrist and staring at her hand. "This is really starting to hurt."

"You should see a doctor. There could be slivers of glass in that cut."

"Let's assume not and treat it like a skinned knee, shall we? It's not deep and I'm not crazy about showing up in the local E.R. and spending a fortune for some doctor to pat me on the head and tell me I'm fine."

"Have you had a tetanus shot lately?"

She pulled a face and arched an eyebrow at him. "Yes."

"Okay. Don't get upset. I'm just trying to help."

"If you really want to help you can follow me to the sink and use that flashlight on this cut so we can see if we spot any shiny glass fragments."

"I'm not a medic."

"No, but you said you were in the Marines. Didn't they teach you first aid?"

"Yes. I guess I can manage—as long as you don't turn around and sue me."

Chancy laughed. "Sue you? Mister, you have definitely lived in the city too long. You're far too jaded for Serenity. Folks around here take care of each other." She started toward the utility sink to wash.

"Like somebody just tried to take care of you?" Nate reminded her, following closely.

"That was an accident, pure and simple."

A shiver tickled her spine all the way from her toes to the roots of her hair when he asked, "Was it?"

"Of course it was. I tripped over the box and broke some glass, that's all."

"Oh?" Pausing, Nate used the beam of the flashlight to highlight the shadowy place where Chancy had landed. "Take a good look."

She was tired from the rigors of the long day and his queries were making her testy in spite of her usually sunny disposition. Still, she followed his instructions. "What? I see the box and the broken glass."

"Exactly," Nate said slowly, as if explaining to a child. "What else do you see?"

"Dust bunnies?" She pouted. "What am I supposed to notice?"

"The position of the box and the glass. They're not together the way they'd be if your fall had caused the breakage. Your hand landed in glass that was a good three feet from the box you tripped over. Unless you dropkicked that box first, there's no way your accident should have moved any glass that far."

"It was broken already?"

"Looks like it to me."

Wide-eyed, she stared from the floor to Nate's face, noting his concern. "Somebody else broke that glass before we got here," she concluded, growing pale.

"I'd say so, yes."

"You think someone was in here?"

"I think chances are very good that the shadow you saw was human, not imaginary, and our arrival interrupted whoever was going through your stuff."

"But, why?"

"I don't know. I do think you should notify the sheriff, though."

"And tell him what? After the wild goose chase I sent him on earlier today, I doubt he'd be thrilled to hear from me again. He sounded pretty miffed when I told him we'd found the van ourselves."

"It's his job to check out possible crimes, Chancy."

"Well, yes, but our sheriff is an elected official. He doesn't have to have passed even one class on law enforcement in order to run for office. All he needs is to get enough votes and he's in. The man who's doing it now is a really nice guy but he's probably not going to be dusting for fingerprints or anything. Not for simple breaking and entering. And certainly not when we have no proof."

"At least you can ask him to keep an eye on the store for you during the night."

That suggestion made Chancy laugh nervously. "I don't think that would help. We have 9-1-1 service and a central dispatcher can call for police help if need be, but nobody is actually on duty in the field from midnight to six in the morning."

Now it was Nate's turn to roll his eyes. "I don't believe this place. What about crime?"

"There isn't any to speak of," she answered.

"Wrong," he said sternly. "Now, there is."

FIVE

To Chancy's relief her cuts had bled enough to cleanse themselves and Nate hadn't found any glass lodged in her palm before he'd bandaged it. That helped her calm down. So did keeping busy unloading the truck and the van with Nate, in spite of his assurances that he wanted to do it all himself.

The thought that her shop might actually have been burglarized, however, remained unsettling. As a result, she was sorry to see their task coming to an end because that meant he'd soon be leaving and she'd be alone.

Nate dusted off his hands. "Well, that's the last of the boxes."

"Yes, I see. Thanks for all your help."

"You're quite welcome."

Chancy assumed, since he was scanning the storeroom, he was still looking for anything amiss. "We've been through this whole place, front and back," she said to reassure him. "Nothing seems to be missing and everything is secure now. It has to be."

"I know." He stuffed his hands into the pockets of his jacket and struck a nonchalant pose. "So, if you're done working let's lock up and I'll see you home."

"That's impossible."

"Why?" He began to scowl. "I'm not making a pass, if that's what you're worried about. I just want to make sure you're okay."

Laughing lightly, Chancy shook her head. "You don't understand. You can't escort me home because I already am home. I have an apartment upstairs."

"Here? In this building? Why didn't you say so?"

"It didn't seem relevant."

"Well, it is. Where's the access?"

"There's a hidden stairway in front, in the retail section, and another one outside like a fire escape."

"Show me."

"That won't be necessary, really, it won't."

Nate was adamant. "Look, Chancy, if you don't want me to do a walk-through of your apartment, then call the sheriff and ask him to do it. Either way is fine with me. But I'm not leaving until somebody checks out your place and makes sure it's safe. Period."

She faced him, hands fisted on her hips. "You're serious?"

"Deadly serious."

It occurred to her that the good Lord might have

led Nate into her life for just such a purpose, although she wasn't keen on sharing that notion with him—or with anyone else. She prided herself on her self-reliance and it galled her to admit the man could actually be right in this instance.

"All right. You can look. But you have to promise to ignore the clutter. I left in a hurry this morning."

"I'm a bachelor. I doubt your place is any more cluttered than mine is."

She led the way to the interior stairway that was camouflaged by a bookcase that swung out on silent hinges. Opening it, she waited for Nate to appreciate its cleverness as much as she did. "Pretty neat, huh?"

His terse "Amazing," sounded more like disgust than approval.

Chancy motioned him to proceed while she continued their earlier conversation. "You have a cleaning lady, don't you?"

"Yes. She comes in twice a week. How did you know?"

"It fit the profile. College grad, city dweller, single guy with a good job. Why should you clean your own house?"

"Exactly."

"Well, I don't have a maid so bear with me, okay?" At the top of the narrow staircase she added, "Go on in."

When Nate opened the door to her apartment she

was immediately sorry to see that she'd left a stack of partially folded laundry on one end of the sofa. Not only that, the dishes hadn't been washed for several days and there was a jumbled pile of unopened mail on the side table beside her favorite rocking chair. The fact that the chair was an original, oak Gustav Stickley with a three-slat back and horsehair-padded seat, circa 1900, didn't make up for the fact that the room it sat in wasn't very tidy.

All business, Nate left her, offering a curt, "Wait here. I'll be right back."

At this point, there was nothing Chancy could do to make a better first impression, so she hung back and let her self-appointed protector do his job and search her apartment.

He returned quickly. "Looks okay to me. Lock your door after I leave and don't let anybody in."

She pressed her lips together and gave him a lopsided smile. "Um, I can't lock this interior door. I don't have a key." She brightened. "But I can lock the one to the fire escape outside."

"Terrific. Okay. We secured the downstairs already. You can let me out up here and lock it behind me."

"Nope." Chancy knew she had to be blushing because her face felt far too warm.

"I beg your pardon?"

"I'd rather let you out downstairs if you don't mind. Otherwise, the neighbors might see you leaving and assume I was entertaining a man in my apartment. Unchaperoned."

"Who would care?"

"Everybody."

"We weren't doing anything we shouldn't."

"That's not the point," she explained. "I don't want to give the wrong impression."

Nate was frowning at her. "You're serious?"

"Oh, yes. As you said recently, I'm deadly serious. Good reputations are very important in Serenity."

"They're important everywhere," he answered. "We certainly wouldn't want yours to suffer simply because you let me out the wrong door."

"When you put it that way, it does sound pretty silly."

"Not really." He was already at the doorway and getting ready to start back down the stairs.

Chancy followed. "I'll have to come along if you want me to bar the back door from the inside the way we discussed. I can't understand why that lock wouldn't catch right when we tried it earlier."

"Probably because it's older than Methuselah," he said over his shoulder.

Or because someone damaged it, she thought.

"Pick up a new one at the hardware store and I'll stop by and install it for you."

There he goes again, assuming I'm helpless. "That won't be necessary. I can do it."

"You're a carpenter, too?"

"When you live in an old building like this one you either get handy or the place falls apart around you," she answered. "But thanks for offering. Give my love to Ted and Hester."

Nate crossed the storage room and paused to free the exit door. "I will. Bar this after me."

She gave a mocking salute and grinned. "Yes, sir!"

Instead of laughing, Nate stepped through and closed the door, then waited, adding a clipped, "Do it."

As soon as Chancy placed the wooden brace across the door and slid it into its brackets, she heard him testing it with a rattle.

"Satisfied?" she called out.

Nate didn't answer. She listened as he started the truck and drove off.

Sighing, she turned to survey her rustic warehouse. It was still brightly lit but for the first time in memory she felt uneasy here.

It wasn't fair. Whoever had violated her private space might not have stolen anything tangible but they had still robbed her. They'd taken her peace of mind.

Nate drove the old green truck slowly through Serenity. He'd forgotten how different life was in such a small town. Sometimes, being there made him feel as if he were caught in a time warp. The streets weren't totally deserted yet but he suspected that the only ones out and about later this Saturday night would be teenagers. Unlike the active city life he was used to, these people truly did figuratively *roll up the sidewalks* at dusk.

Cruising past the closed drugstore, he noticed that there was a grouping of randomly angled vehicles in the parking lot and kids were standing around outside them as if they were having a meeting. He supposed gathering in public like that was better than some of the other kinds of mischief they could be getting into.

It was hard for Nate to remember ever having been a similarly carefree teen. Even back then he'd been overly serious, intent on standing up for himself and making a success of his life no matter what.

And he had done exactly that, he assured himself. The military had helped him finish his formal education and he had a good job, a nice place to live, friends with whom he spent what little free time he had. So why was he feeling as if there was something missing?

His mind refused to quiet. He thought of Chancy, of the time he'd just spent with her and his grandparents. All three of them seemed to possess a sense of peace that eluded him. Perhaps their apparent contentment was the result of living such a simple life. Nate didn't know. Nor did he intend to spend a lot of time contemplating it.

The only thing he was certain of was that his grandparents had taken him into their home and had loved him unconditionally when his hard-hearted parents had thrown him out. If Ted and Hester hadn't stepped up and vouched for him at that time, he would have been incarcerated in a juvenile detention facility instead. He owed those two old people everything. And he intended to repay them. Soon.

Cruising past Serenity Chapel, he was suddenly struck by the memory of Chancy's remark that she attended church on Sundays and he wondered if this was where she worshipped. Not that it made any difference. He had, however, considered that one method of influencing his grandparents might be to involve their pastor in his long-range plans. If someone they both respected were to side with Nate about their future, he figured he'd have a better chance of getting them to pack up and move to Oklahoma.

In the meantime, since he was in the neighborhood, he was going to stop by the sheriff's office and mention that Chancy's place needed watching, whether she thought so or not.

He swung around the courthouse square, past the hardware store and chamber of commerce, then parked in one of the many empty diagonal slots in front of the county offices.

An older man with a paunch that strained his

beige uniform shirt and a mustache thick enough to double as a whisk broom was sitting on the front stoop, smoking.

He stood, stomped out his stub of a cigarette and hoisted his gun belt to straighten it as Nate approached. "Help ya?"

"I hope so, Sheriff. I'm Nate Collins. Ted and Hester's grandson," he said, aware of how important familial identification was in a place like Serenity.

The lawman smiled and shook his hand. "Well, well. I heard you was back in town. Should of recognized old Ted's truck. What brings you to see me?"

Nodding in the general direction of the antique shop Nate said, "I think you should keep an eye on Chancy's Second Chances. I suspect there was a break-in there tonight."

"We didn't get a call, did we?"

"No. She didn't want you to think she was crying wolf, especially after her van turned up back at the Hawkins place earlier today. But I think there was somebody in her shop."

"What makes you say that?"

"Several things," Nate said. "The back door was unlocked when we got there and she was sure she'd locked it. Plus, when we tried to secure the door later, the lock wouldn't catch. It acted as if it had been sprung."

"Did you see anybody?"

"Chancy thought she did, but she's not positive. It was dark and the only other sign of illegal entry was some broken glass and a box that had evidently been moved."

"Mighty little to go on," the sheriff said.

"I know. But it wouldn't hurt to cruise by once in a while, would it?"

"S'pose not." He checked his watch. "I go off duty in a few minutes. I can drive that route on my way home."

Cautious, not wanting to rile the lawman, Nate managed a smile before remarking, "I heard there was no one minding your office at night. That seems kind of unusual to me."

The sheriff guffawed and spat over the side of the steps into the dirt. "That's 'cause you're not from around here, son."

Nate's smile widened. "I've heard that said before."

"Undoubtedly. And you'll probably hear it again. I imagine Miss Hester's real glad to have you visit, though. How long you stayin'?"

"I don't know, exactly."

"Well, don't you fret about Chancy's place. I'll take a look-see and tell my deputy to do the same. Girl like that, all alone the way she is, needs protectin'."

"Did you know her parents?" Nate asked.

Sobering, the older man nodded and sighed. "That, I did. Broke up many a fight at their place before it blew clean away. Those two used to squabble like a couple a fightin' roosters cooped up in the same little pen."

"Grandma Hester says they were killed together, too."

"That they were. Tornado come down and made kindlin' of their whole house. There was a warning given but they apparently figured it didn't apply to them so they ignored it." He snorted derisively. "I felt sorry for the girl but those folks of hers made my life a misery, sure enough. It was so quiet for a while after their funeral I hardly knew what to do with all my spare time."

"Chancy wasn't around when it happened?"

"Nope." He shook his head slowly. "She'd moved out and opened her shop in town. We were all glad to see her on her own, what with the fights and all goin' on at home. I heard she blamed herself for not bein' there but that's pure nonsense."

"Survivor's guilt," Nate said with understanding and empathy. "It's pretty typical."

"Whatever. Well, if I'm gonna check on her I'd best be going." Once again he shook Nate's hand. "Tell your grandma I still love her chocolate-chip cookies. She can bring me some anytime she pleases."

"You take bribes?" Nate quipped.

"If they taste good enough I do," he answered, grinning and patting his ample girth.

Nate was still smiling and shaking his head as he climbed back into the pickup and headed for his grandparents' farmhouse. Obviously, the good old boy network that had given him so much personal grief years ago was still alive and well. The good part was it no longer bothered him to be considered an outsider. On the contrary, he was relieved to have moved beyond teenage angst and into self-reliant adulthood. He wasn't upset that he didn't fit in. He was grateful.

"I got two of my collages back, Sam." The nervous young woman gripped the telephone receiver with both hands to keep it from shaking.

"What about the other one? You told me you sold three out of four of them."

"I did." She eased her thin body down on the edge of the unmade bed and tried to keep from sounding as worried as she really was. "And I know where the last one is. All I have to do is get my hands on it and then I'll have all your keys back."

"If you can't buy it, steal it. Just don't get caught."

"I've been working on that," she said. "I almost had it."

"*Almost* doesn't cut it," he warned. "I told you what to do. Now do it."

"I will, Sam. I promise." She paused, then changed the subject. "How've you been?"

He cursed. "How do you think I've been? If I wasn't due to get out of here in a few more days I'd go crazy. I'm halfway there as it is."

The truth of his statement gave her the shivers. "Do you want me to come to Forrest City to pick you up when you're released? I think the car will make it okay."

"No. I've already made other arrangements. Where are you living now, Little Rock or Sherwood?"

"Neither. I moved away after…after the trouble. I got a place about three hours north of there, just outside a little town called Serenity."

"Well, get back down to Little Rock."

"I—I can't. Not until I get my collage back."

He cursed again, making her skin crawl. "Okay. As long as you have your cell phone and I can get in touch with you, that'll have to do. See that you keep it turned on all the time. Understand? I don't want any slipups. Once you get those keys we'll talk about where we should meet."

"Okay."

Hanging up, she felt tears fill her eyes and start to trickle down her cheeks. If she thought for one second she could escape Sam's control, she'd do it. In a heartbeat. But that was impossible. She'd fallen for him and married him before she'd seen his true character and now it was too late to go back. Too late to save herself.

SIX

Sunday had dawned bright and promising. No amount of fatigue or sore muscles from time spent at the auction site could have kept Chancy home from church on a day so perfect for praising the Lord. It was as if all of nature was singing hymns and yesterday's troubles were ancient history.

She had taken the makeshift bandage off her hand when she'd showered that morning and was pleased to note that the cut no longer looked as if it needed to be covered. Good. The last thing she wanted was to be called upon to explain her injury.

An uneasy feeling had kept trying to rise from her subconscious as she'd put on her favorite blue dress but she'd pushed her worry down, unwilling to allow anyone or anything to steal her joy.

During the drive to Serenity Chapel she'd kept telling herself that God was in control, although, she acknowledged that she'd often had problems accepting His infinite wisdom, especially where her parents were concerned. That was the trouble with faith. Fallible human beings were always questioning things, especially those things over which they had no control, and she was as human as anyone.

Serenity Chapel stood on a rise at the edge of town, its white steeple visible above the treetops. The building itself was constructed of neat-looking brick and bordered by a simple garden but it was the steeple that called to Chancy as she approached.

Some people had speculated that a church that big and imposing would be off-putting to strangers, yet she knew once they came inside and experienced being a part of the friendly, loving congregation, they'd discover that their misgivings were unfounded.

Pastor Logan Malloy was standing just inside the glass doors at the front, welcoming parishioners, when Chancy arrived. His wife Becky stood beside him, all smiles.

Chancy shook Logan's hand and gave Becky a hug as she returned their morning greetings. "Hello, you two. Where's the baby? In the nursery?"

Becky nodded. "Yes. Aunt Effie's on duty in there today. She was waiting for us when we drove up. You know how crazy she is about babies. She couldn't wait to get her hands on little Timothy."

Chancy shook her head. "Well, more power to her. Children scare me to death."

"I used to feel the same way," Becky answered. "But now it's hard to imagine my life before Timmy arrived."

Others were pressing in behind Chancy, spurring her to move on. "Well, I guess I'd better be going. Will you be at the women's group tea later this month?"

Becky grinned and laughed lightly. "I'd better be. Last I heard it was going to be at my house."

"Good reason to be there, then. Talk to you later."

Chancy proceeded to Miss Louella's Extraordinary Ladies' Sunday School Class where she knew she'd find many of her dearest friends.

Always a blessing, the popular class had grown a lot in the past few months but it still contained a core of old-timers whose love and concern shone through, no matter who else joined.

Louella was the only one in the room that early. She greeted Chancy with a motherly hug. "Good to see you! I was so worried yesterday."

"It all turned out fine, as I told you when I phoned," Chancy reminded her. "We got the van back and everything was still in it."

"Praise the Lord!"

"I did," Chancy said with a grin. "Lots."

One of Louella's reddish brown eyebrows arched and she smiled as if she was in on a secret. "And by the looks of things you had plenty to praise Him for. I heard you were seen racing all over town in the company of a very handsome man."

"That was Nate Collins, Hester's grandson," she explained, blushing. "He was just helping me look for my missing van."

"And?"

"And nothing," Chancy insisted. "Well, almost nothing. I did get invited to supper at Ted and Hester's."

"With Nate, I take it."

"Of course. He was visiting them and—"

"Aha! I knew it." Louella was clapping her hands, her bangle bracelets jingling. "Tell me everything."

"There's nothing else to tell."

She cast a sidelong glance at the classroom door as Trudy Lynn Keringhoven and Carol Sue Grabowski entered, chatting animatedly and preceding a group of seven or eight others.

Chancy didn't mind airing her concerns or sharing answers to prayer in front of the women she'd known for a long time, but opening up in front of newcomers bothered her enough to keep her from going on with her story, even at Louella's urging.

"Later, then," Louella said behind her hand. "Call me at home."

Without answering directly, Chancy settled into her usual row, placed her purse on the floor by her feet, smoothed her skirt and rested her Bible on her lap. The room was quickly filling up and, as she'd already noted, there were several women with whom she wasn't acquainted.

Louella took command and made necessary introductions. The first person she indicated was a matronly, gray-haired lady with a winning smile and enough wrinkles to make Chancy feel like a teenager.

"I'd like you all to meet Alice Franks," the teacher said. "She's from down south but her people are from around here so she's not really a flatlander."

Chancy and the others greeted Alice with a confusing gaggle of well wishes, hellos and chuckles.

"And this is Melody Smith," Louella went on, indicating a dark-haired woman who appeared to be in her late twenties or early thirties. "She's from Fort Smith. No relation to the town, right, dear?"

"No, ma'am."

Louella turned to the other newcomer whose age and coloring was quite similar to Melody's. "And last but not least, this is Joanna Jones. Hey, we have a Smith and a Jones now! How interesting. You two ladies look enough alike to be sisters. Had you ever met before?"

Joanna shook her head, lowering her eyes to her lap as if she wished she'd chosen to attend a more staid class. Chancy could understand her reticence. The women in the Extraordinary Ladies' Class were unique, both in their openness and in their ability to find something they all wanted to talk about no matter what the situation. That kind of powerful group dynamic could be a bit overwhelming to anyone who wasn't used to it.

Sizing up the two young women, Chancy was struck by more than their similarity of appearance. There was also a shared sense of reserve. Perhaps there was some deep-seated reason why each of them needed prayer.

Once they'd heard how others in the class broached sensitive subjects she hoped they would speak up, too. It wasn't necessary to ask for specific things when requesting group prayer. It was enough to simply say there was an unspoken need and leave it at that.

And in the meantime, Chancy thought, she would pray silently for her newly met sisters to the Lord. After all, it was the prayers of the faithful that had upheld her during the trauma of losing her parents. The least she could do was repay that kindness with intercession of her own.

Nate had decided at the last minute to accompany his grandparents to church. Judging by the astonished expression on his grandmother's face when he'd announced his intentions, his willingness to go had surprised her almost as much as it had surprised him. Ted and Hester had tried to get him involved in the local church as a teen but he'd always found plenty of reasons to beg off. This morning, however, he couldn't seem to convince himself to stay home.

Rationalizing his choice by recalling his desire to

speak with their pastor, he had stopped arguing with himself, had dressed accordingly and had come down to breakfast wearing his best slacks and sport coat.

"I didn't bring a tie," Nate had said when Hester had openly admired his outfit.

"Bah. I wouldn't go if I had to choke myself to death to do it," Ted had replied. "You don't need no necktie. All you need is to show up with the best you've got. Folks that don't have much are just as welcome as those bankers and such with their fancy suits and shiny shoes. I wouldn't be a part of a church that shunned people because of their duds."

Therefore, Nate had relaxed and had accompanied the elderly couple, which was why he was now seated in a front pew and wishing he could move to the rear where hopefully he wouldn't be attracting quite so much attention. He'd had to jump up so often to greet the members of the congregation that his grandmother kept introducing, he was beginning to feel like a kid on a pogo stick.

He'd just finished making polite conversation with a couple who looked to be about his grandparents' age when he glanced up the aisle and saw a face he recognized. Chancy was here. She *did* go to this church.

"I didn't know that, of course," he muttered, intent on convincing himself he hadn't decided to come this morning on the off chance he'd run into her.

Ted's eyes followed Nate's and settled on the

pretty golden-haired woman in the sky-blue dress. "Well, well. Lookie who's here." He elbowed Nate. "You ought to go say hello, maybe sit back there with her, don't you think, son?"

"I came with you and Grandma."

"We aren't goin' anywhere. We'll still be sittin' right here when the service is over. Now, scoot. Before that there pew fills up and you lose your chance."

"I would like to see how she's doing today," Nate said. "She was pretty upset last night."

Ted gave him a friendly nudge. "Go on."

Feeling his face warming with unexpected embarrassment, Nate started up the aisle toward Chancy.

When she looked up, smiled and raised her hand to wave, he could hardly believe how elated he was over such a simple gesture.

Chancy was so glad to see Nate she almost forgot herself and gave him the same kind of welcoming hug with which she'd already greeted many of her local friends. Observing the Southern custom of embracing was fine under the proper circumstances. In Nate's case, however, she felt it would be wiser to hold back. There were bound to be enough rumors circulating about her after yesterday's events involving him and she didn't want to add fuel to the fires of gossip by hugging the man in front of the entire congregation.

But, oh, was she happy to see him! Her grin spread

so wide her cheek muscles hurt and she couldn't have kept the joy out of her voice if she'd tried when she said, "Hello!"

Nate returned her smile. "Hello. How did it go last night?"

Bless his heart, he hadn't said, "After I left," in public, Chancy thought with relief. "Fine. Everything was peaceful."

"Glad to hear it."

They were standing to one side of the main aisle but partially blocking it nonetheless, so they edged over farther.

"Did you come with Ted and Hester?" Chancy asked, peering past him to scan the front of the sanctuary where the couple usually sat.

"Yes."

"Well, in that case, I won't ask you to sit back here. I don't want to hurt their feelings."

Nate hesitated instead of returning to his family. "That shouldn't be a problem."

"Oh. Well, if you're sure?"

What else could she say? It was wonderful to see Nate again and if he wanted to sit by her, so much the better. She'd intended to invite him to church herself and had failed to find the perfect opportunity so she'd held back. Now that the Lord had apparently used some other method to get him in the door, however, she wasn't quite sure what she should do.

Sitting down would be good, her logical side answered. *And stop grinning like a fool!*

She slipped into the nearest pew, careful to leave room for Nate to join her. When he did, the room suddenly seemed too warm, the air insufficient.

What is wrong with me, Lord? she prayed silently. *I'm not a silly, impressionable teenager anymore, so why do I feel like one?*

Because Nate is special, she concluded without waiting for word from above. That absolute truth shook her to the core. He was special. To her. The question was, what was she going to do about it?

Clasping her hands in her lap atop her Bible, Chancy forced herself to calm down. It had been a long, long time since she'd had romantic notions about any man, let alone one as handsome as Nate Collins. Assuming she wasn't imagining things, what was going on? Was God trying to tell or show her something? It would be lovely to think so, wouldn't it?

Nervous, she filled the silence before the service began with quiet chatter, leaning closer to ask, "How are Hester and Ted?"

"Very well, thanks." He gave her a lopsided smile. "I did think Grandma was going to faint when I told her I wanted to come with them this morning. I didn't bring a suit but Ted said this jacket was okay."

"It's fine."

Better than fine, on you, Chancy added silently,

hoping she hadn't sounded too enthusiastic. The man obviously had no idea how great he looked or how much attention he was attracting. Even women Louella's age and older had been giving him the once-over and Chancy found herself feeling surprisingly jealous.

"So, tell me more about your job," she said. "Do you work for a TV station or something like that?"

"No," Nate replied. "I'm based at the National Weather Forecast Office in Norman, Oklahoma, but I spend a lot of my time in the field."

"Really? Doing what, standing out there with your hand in the air so you can feel if it's raining?"

That comment made him laugh even though it had sounded inane to her the minute she'd uttered it.

"No," Nate said with a subdued chuckle, "although that is a pretty good idea. Actually, I'm on a crew that takes a Doppler On Wheels unit to wherever the worst storms are."

"Storms?" She was starting to get a very uneasy feeling.

"Yes. We chase them, gather data and process it," he said. "The worse they are, the better we like it."

"You're not talking about regular rain, are you?"

"No. Tornadoes are what we mostly look for, although super cells can produce hail, rain and dangerous straight-line winds, as well."

Chancy felt as if some of that hail he'd been talking about had just clobbered her between the eyes. *Of course.* Everything he'd said at dinner the evening before had pointed to it but she'd been too bumfuzzled and too enthralled to catch on.

Eyes widening, she gaped at him. "You chase tornadoes? For fun?"

"Yes. It's my job. I thought you knew."

"How would I?"

He shrugged. "I just assumed…"

Inching away from him as if he were contagious, she had to consciously force herself to stay seated rather than bolt and run for the door. Nothing frightened her more than the idea of being overtaken by a tornado and being buried alive the way her parents had been. To think that Nate would deliberately place himself in harm's way was enough to turn her stomach.

"How can you do that to Hester?" Chancy whispered, barely able to breathe, let alone speak.

"How can I do *what* to her? I'm part of a scientific team that's trying to learn enough to predict what conditions severe storms will produce and ultimately save lives, Chancy. I'd think you, of all people, would appreciate that."

Chastened, she nodded. "I suppose I should. It's just that…"

"What?"

"Nothing. It's not important." She pointed demurely. "Shush. There's Brother Logan. The service is starting."

Saved from further conversation by the entrance of the choir and Logan Malloy at the front of the sanctuary, Chancy withdrew into herself.

She still couldn't bear to watch news footage of tornadoes on TV. No way was she going to allow herself to get to know Nate better and wind up thinking of him, worrying about him, every time she heard another report of tornado damage or possible loss of life. She couldn't start to care about him. She wouldn't. It was unthinkable to even consider getting involved with someone like him.

Thank you, Father, that I found out in time, she prayed silently with her hands clenched in her lap. Humiliating tears misted her vision and threatened to spill out. She bit the inside of her lip to distract herself and hold them back.

Why, oh, why, hadn't she asked the specifics of Nate's occupation in time to keep from liking him, from growing fond of him? She was already more concerned about his future welfare than she cared to be and she didn't know how she was going to change that—or if it was even possible.

One thing was certain. She was *not* going to have anything more to do with him. Nothing. Nada. Zilch. She didn't care if he was the sweetest, best-looking man in Serenity, she wasn't going to let herself fall for him. No sirree.

The congregation stood to sing the opening hymn. On Chancy's left, Nate's rich baritone swelled with such God-given talent it sent a shiver skittering along her spine.

In spite of her vows to ignore him, she was caught up in the singing, in the sound of his voice, in the sense of his continued presence. What was wrong with her? Was she out of her mind?

No. Nate was the one who had to be mentally unbalanced, not her. And the sooner she got away from him the better off she'd be.

Her feet shifted. She eyed the aisle. The only things keeping her from fleeing were her inbred Southern manners and her desire to truly worship the Lord.

Nobody, not even a meteorologist with an apparent death wish, was going to rob her of either of those.

SEVEN

Nate was seated next to the aisle so Chancy had to pass him in order to leave at the end of the morning service. He wanted to do or say something that would alleviate the tension between them but he couldn't think of a single thing.

Even her polite "excuse me," as she picked up her purse and Bible and prepared to leave seemed strained to him. Perhaps it was. The electricity in the air around them felt as charged as that which often preceded a lightning storm.

"Then I guess this is goodbye?" he asked.

She didn't meet his gaze as she sidled past him but she did at least nod.

He stepped aside, astonished to see her heading for the exit without delay. He supposed he should have known how she'd react once she was apprised of his passion for storms, but her evident aversion to him, as a person, was still a bit of a shock.

Well, that couldn't be helped. He was what he was. And if this morning's sermon was to be believed, that diversity was okay with God. Unfortunately, it didn't seem to be okay with Chancy Boyd.

He waited until Ted and Hester made their way up the aisle and joined him.

Ted raised an eyebrow. "Where'd she go?"

"Who?" Nate asked, knowing full well what his grandfather meant.

"That pretty gal you was sittin' with. What'd you do, make Chancy mad?"

"Actually, I think I scared her when I mentioned my job," Nate said soberly.

"You should have known better," Hester chimed in. "I warned you how she felt about things like that."

"That doesn't change what I do for a living. Besides, there's no harm done. I won't be around here much longer, anyway, so it's just as well."

"More's the pity," Hester said, taking Nate's arm as they walked toward the door of the sanctuary with Ted bringing up the rear. "We have tornadoes here, too, you know. You could always stay in Arkansas and chase ours."

Nate patted her hand. "Sorry. I need to be in the plains where I can see what's coming and move around faster. I would like to be closer to you and Grandpa though, to be able to look after you. That's the reason I want you to move to Oklahoma."

"There he goes again," Ted grumbled. "Sounds like a broken record the way he repeats himself." He snorted derisively. "'Course, time will come when nobody knows what a broken record is, now that everybody's got them CDs and little music thingamabobs hangin' from their ears."

Nate chuckled quietly. He knew from experience that his grandfather's grumpiness was mostly an act. Underneath that crusty exterior was a loving heart unlike that of any other man he'd ever known. How Charles Collins, Nate's harsh, dictatorial father, could have been Ted's offspring had never ceased to amaze. Charles allowed no mistakes and forgave nothing. The only thing Nate was glad about was that he'd had no siblings so no other child had had to grow up under his father's roof.

"Let's all go out to eat," Hester piped up. "I don't fancy cookin' today."

"Well," Ted drawled, winking at Nate, "I don't know. I kinda had my mouth set for one of your special Sunday dinners, Mama."

"It'll be my treat," Nate said. "Where would you like to go? How about Bea's Café, on the square? They've got good home-cooked food and you've always liked their pies."

"I s'pose it'll do," Ted conceded. "Beats starvin' to death while your grandma pouts because she didn't get to go to a restaurant like she wanted."

Hester took a playful swipe at her husband and lightly whacked his arm as they neared the door where Logan Malloy was bidding his parishioners goodbye. "Hush, Ted. You'll have the preacher thinkin' I'm a poor wife."

Logan took her hand and shook it gently. "Never you mind him, Miss Hester. Ted knows he's got a prize. He just likes to tease you."

Standing back, Nate watched the exchange between his grandparents and their pastor with interest. Clearly, Logan Malloy thought a lot of the older couple, and they of him. Therefore, enlisting his help might be the best next step. It certainly wouldn't hurt to at least approach him and ask to discuss Hester and Ted's welfare.

When it was Nate's turn to shake Logan's hand he paused just long enough to ask, "May I drop in sometime in the next few days and talk to you?"

"Of course." Logan clasped Nate's hand with both of his and shook it vigorously. "Be glad to see you. Far as I know, tomorrow morning is open. I usually do hospital visitations on Tuesdays."

"Good. I'll see you tomorrow morning, then."

His grandparents had gone on ahead so Nate hurried to catch up with them. Ted had helped Hester into the cab of the truck and was getting in beside her when Nate slid behind the wheel.

"Well," Ted commented with a grin, "you look

mighty pleased with yourself. Did you locate Chancy again?"

Nate scowled. "No. What gave you that idea? I wasn't even looking for her."

"Too bad," Ted said. "I thought sure you'd want to help her change that flat tire."

The key was halfway to the ignition. Nate froze. "Flat tire? She has a flat tire?" He scanned the parking lot. "Where? I didn't see her van."

By this time Ted was guffawing and Hester was smacking him on the back of the hand. She smiled at her grandson. "We didn't see hide nor hair of her and your grandpa knows it. Start the truck and let's go, son. I'm hungry and Bea's is only open till two o'clock on Sundays."

Setting his jaw, Nate knew he'd given away his true feelings with regard to Chancy Boyd. Well, so what? She was obviously not interested in getting to know him any better and that was just as well. Not only were their lives worlds apart, they were also not in tune spiritually. She gave credit to God for even the smallest things while he felt personally responsible for whatever happened, good or bad.

Take the way he had turned his life around, for instance. He, Nate Collins, had done that, not God. *Right?*

His attention was drawn to the two dear people

seated beside him. Their positive influence deserved some credit, too, of course.

And who or what brought you into their care?

Nate was taken aback. Where had that thought come from? He shook off the notion of divine intervention and willed himself to concentrate more on his driving. He'd always felt fortunate that he'd been able to come to live with his grandparents at a critical time of his young life but it had never before occurred to him that perhaps his destiny had been molded for the better by powers beyond his own understanding.

Although that should have been a comforting thought, Nate found it extremely disquieting.

Chancy had ducked into Louella's classroom when she'd noticed that her friend had gone back there to straighten up after the worship service.

"Hi," she said, leaving the door ajar.

"Hey! Chancy. Glad you stopped in. I wanted to ask you more about the man you were with this morning. He is one great-looking guy. No wonder you spent so much time together yesterday."

"It's not what you think. Nate came to church with his grandparents and just happened to sit near me."

"Horse feathers," Louella said with a giggle. "Hester and Ted were way up front by the pulpit."

"I'm friends with the Collins family, that's all."

"I know you are, dear. And I think it was sweet of

you to give Hester all those pictures you bought at the Hawkins auction."

"How did you know about them?"

"Heard it through the grapevine," Louella said. "You know, you'll never get rich if you give stuff away before you even try to sell it."

"I know. But Hester wanted something to remember Jewel and Pete by and I figured the pictures would be a good way to do that. All I wanted was the antique frames, anyway. It's no great loss to me, even if she decides to keep them all."

So, that's why I couldn't find my collage, the eavesdropper in the church hallway thought. *She must have given it away! Now what am I going to do?*

Tears welled in her dark eyes and she blinked them back. All was not lost. Actually, locating the small artwork item in a home would probably be easier than trying to find it in Chancy's crammed warehouse.

Leaning against the wall next to the slightly open classroom door, she listened for more clues to the recipient of the valuable collage. None came. Well, it had still been worthwhile to come to this church in order to hang around Chancy and listen to her conversations. She'd overheard the names Hester and Collins. That should be sufficient information for the next step in her quest.

And if it isn't?

If it wasn't, she'd start asking around until she found out exactly who had wound up with the picture. These church people were a trusting lot. They'd probably even give her the collage if she told them a sad enough story. Hopefully, that wouldn't be necessary because it might make somebody ask too many questions and thereby expose her to possible discovery.

The last thing she wanted to do was focus anyone's attention on the keys she'd glued onto the collage with the old jewelry. Precious keys. Sam's keys.

The thought of her husband made her shiver. He'd be out soon. He'd want to come home to her. To the life they'd led before he'd been sent to jail.

Remembrance was enough to cause a few tears to spill out and slide down her cheeks. Swiping them away she hurried toward the side exit, her efforts at spying on Chancy abandoned, and literally bumped into a middle-aged woman who looked slightly familiar.

"Excuse me," the eavesdropper said.

"No problem, dear." The older woman was temporarily blocking her escape. "Say, are you all right?"

"Fine." Sniffling, she fought to create an unruffled image in spite of her inner turbulence.

"Well, then, I won't detain you. I can see you're in a hurry. Don't you worry. I'm new here, too, and I know how hard it is to fit in when you feel like an outsider."

"I'm sorry. I don't recall exactly…"

"I'm Alice. Alice Franks. We met in Sunday-school class this morning. I'll be sure to look for you next week." She started to back away. "You have a lovely day, y'hear. Bye-bye, now."

"Goodbye."

Relieved, the eavesdropper again started to make a beeline for the nearest exit. Just then, a grand-motherly type with curly gray hair and twinkling blue eyes popped out of the nursery and confronted her with a smile.

"Hello there. Have you seen Becky? She's the preacher's wife. Her baby's getting awfully fussy and I think he's hungry. Would you mind running up to the front and asking her to hurry? Tell her Aunt Effie sent you."

"I—I really can't, I…"

Before she could break away and complete her escape, the old woman had joined her in the hallway and embraced her gently. "I'm so sorry, dear. Never mind. I didn't notice that you were upset. Is there anything I can do to help?"

"No. Nothing. I'm fine, really."

"Of course you are. Just remember, Jesus knows your troubles and He's ready to help anytime you call on Him."

Biting back tears, the dark-haired young woman pulled away. As she was passing through the doorway to the parking lot she heard Effie call, "Don't worry. I'll pray for you."

Deeply touched, she swiped at her now flowing tears. It had been a mistake to come to church again after so many years away. It reminded her of happier times, of people who cared about each other even if they were new to the congregation, of the kind of loving family she'd once had and had thrown away.

Her friends and family hadn't liked Sam in the first place and her decision to marry him had caused a terrible rift. One that had proved insurmountable.

It was nice of the old lady to offer to pray for her but it wouldn't do any good. She knew it wouldn't. She'd prayed and prayed for a second chance and it had never come. She hadn't expected it to.

Nate had stayed in Serenity longer than he'd planned to in order to visit with Logan Malloy, as promised. He had come away from their meeting disgusted and disheartened. Not only was the pastor noncommittal about whether or not Ted and Hester could take care of themselves, his solution to the problem had been to suggest that the church do more to help, rather than encourage them to sell their farm and move away.

In the days that followed, Nate had helped Ted repair the barn roof and porch railing, then had taken his leave.

Now that he was in the air and flying west, he had time to reflect on all that had transpired during his short visit. It certainly hadn't been boring, had it?

The easiest thing to picture was Chancy's face, with those freckles across her nose and the little dimples in her cheeks that only showed up when she smiled—which was most of the time.

He shook off the memory. There were plenty of available women in and around Norman if he ever decided to get serious about settling down. As it was, he was torn between his job and his private life. Any future mate he considered would have to be more than tolerant of his dedication to his profession.

Besides, if his parents' frosty relationship was an example of a normal marriage, he wasn't interested. He didn't want merely a housemate, he wanted a soul mate. Someone like Hester was to Ted.

Therefore, such a union was possible, Nate reasoned. As long as he stayed focused on what he wanted in a wife—or, more importantly what he *didn't* want—he'd recognize the right person when she came along.

The image of Chancy's smiling face popped into his mind once again. He set his jaw in consternation. Hopefully, he wouldn't have to return to Serenity soon. The less contact he had to have with that particular woman, the better off he knew he'd be.

Chancy was at work the following week when she received a panicky call from Hester Collins. The elderly woman was so upset she was almost incoherent.

"Whoa. Calm down, Miss Hester," Chancy said. "Whatever it is, I know it can be fixed. Tell me again what happened."

"The pictures. Jewel and Pete's pictures. They're all gone! Every one!"

Scowling, Chancy gripped the receiver and wondered if she'd heard correctly. "The pictures I gave you are gone?"

"Yes. All of 'em. I left 'em on the coffee table by the sofa and the next thing I knew, they'd disappeared. I thought maybe you'd picked 'em up."

"No. I gave those to you. I wouldn't have taken back a gift. And I certainly wouldn't have done anything like that without asking permission first."

"Well, I didn't think so but…"

"Is anything else missing?"

"Not that I can tell. Ted's lookin' the place over now."

"Was the house broken in to?"

Hester snorted derisively. "Couldn't of been. You know we never lock our doors."

"Surely Domino would have barked to let you know if a stranger came by."

"Don't know if he did or not. It's the first of the month. Pension day. We went to town to get our groceries just like we always do and stopped by the bank to pick up some spending money. Couldn't of been gone more 'n an hour or two."

"All right," Chancy said. "Call the sheriff and report the theft. I'll be right over."

"Don't put yourself out. I just needed to ask if you'd taken the pictures so I'd know if they were really missing."

"And they are," Chancy countered, "so something is definitely wrong. Hang up and phone the sheriff right away."

"Oh, I can't do that. Ted'd have my hide if I called the law. He didn't vote for old Harlan and he's never been real happy to see him as sheriff."

"Okay. We'll think of something else, then. Stay close to Ted in case there's a prowler still hanging around. I'll be over as soon as I can lock up."

"I probably just misplaced the pictures because I was lettin' my mind wander," Hester said. "I was poking through the stack and I found this real pretty little jewelry thing, all framed and everything. You'd love it. I'm sure you didn't mean to give it to me."

"If it was in with the other pictures then it's

yours, regardless," Chancy assured her. "Was it stolen, too?"

"No," Hester said. "I was gonna hang it in the bathroom till Ted pitched a fit about it bein' too frilly to suit him. I stuck it in a closet for the time being."

"Then we know that couldn't have been what the thief was after or he wouldn't have taken the others."

"I suppose not." She sighed. "Okay, dear, if you want to come over, come ahead. I baked another batch of those cookies like I made for Nate. We can have a cup of tea and eat them while Ted fumes and fusses. It'll be nice to have your company, especially if I truly did misplace those pictures the way my husband thinks I did."

Bidding Hester goodbye, Chancy quickly made the rounds of her shop, securing it with more care than she usually took. This rash of crime was making her feel terribly vulnerable even though, except for the theft of her van, it basically consisted of petty crimes. What in the world was happening to her peaceful little sanctuary of a town?

She murmured a prayer as she hurried to her van. "Please, God, keep Hester and Ted safe." Glancing back at her shop, she added, "And me, too."

Nate was at the forecast office in Norman, checking long-range reports, when his pager beeped. He peered at the number. It was his grandparents'.

Worried, he immediately returned their call. To his surprise, a strange woman's voice said, "Collins residence."

"Who is this?"

"Oh, Nate, thanks for calling back. This is Chancy Boyd. I'm at the farm with Ted and Hester."

"What's wrong? What happened?"

"A burglary, I think."

"Did anybody get hurt?"

"No. Everybody's fine. They're upstairs checking the bedrooms to see what might be missing."

He sagged onto the edge of his desk with a noisy sigh. "You scared ten years off my life."

"Sorry. I wouldn't have bothered you but I think there's something awfully odd going on around here and Ted refuses to involve the sheriff."

"Sounds like you."

"I had a better reason than the fact that I didn't vote for him. Besides, you did it anyway. Harlan stopped by the store the other day and told me all about your visit."

"Somebody had to take action."

"Exactly my point in calling you," Chancy said. "I think you need to be here, at least for a little while, if you can get away again. I'm really getting concerned."

"What happened?"

He listened while she explained. If there hadn't been all the other strange goings-on recently, he might have scoffed at the report of the missing photos. Under the present circumstances, however, he was entertaining the same niggling fears that Chancy was.

"All right," Nate said. "The powers that be won't like it but I'll try to arrange to take a week or two of my vacation and be there as soon as I can. Don't tell anybody I'm coming. Grandma always wears herself out fussing when she knows she's having company. There's no need for her to go to all that extra work."

"Okay." She paused. "And Nate? Thanks."

He bid her goodbye, then raked his fingers through his hair to vent his frustration. So much for vowing he'd stay away from Serenity and from the young woman who had become so much a part of his recent thoughts.

Well, it couldn't be helped. His grandparents needed him and he was going to their aid. Period. He was a grown man. Surely, he could manage to handle two old people and one meddlesome antique dealer without losing his cool.

EIGHT

Broken glass, torn photographs and cracked frames littered the apartment floor. A young woman sat in the only chair and stared at the mess as tears streaked her face and dropped, unnoticed, onto her faded T-shirt. She'd expended so much energy acting out her anger and frustration that she was totally exhausted.

Sam was out of jail and already asking for a meeting, while she was no closer to retrieving his lost keys than she had been when she'd first learned of her error.

"I should have known it couldn't be that easy when I saw the pile of old frames sitting there in plain sight," she told herself, sniffling. They were the same ones from the auction. She knew they were because she recognized the people pictured in the snapshot on top.

What she should have noticed at the time she stole

them was the absence of anything quite thick enough to be her missing collage. If the old dog on the porch hadn't been barking so fiercely she'd have stopped to check before taking the whole stack. As it was, she'd been so afraid that a neighbor would hear the ruckus and come to investigate that she'd simply grabbed everything, stuffed it into a pillowcase she'd brought for ease of transport and had run out the back door to avoid the dog.

She kicked at one of the broken frames with the toe of her sneaker. It was very similar to the one she'd used on the collage, with filigreed corners and a dark mahogany stain to make it look antique.

"It was a natural mistake," she murmured. "How was I to know?"

Disgusted, she sniffed again. "I'm a lousy crook, that's all. Sam wouldn't have gotten scared. He'd have made sure he had the right thing before he left."

And maybe he'd have gotten caught, again, she added with a shiver. Sam was bold but he wasn't all that smart, was he? Then again, how smart was she? She'd married him in the first place.

Nate circled the landing field. A light brown van was waiting off to one side, near the transient parking for visiting fliers. Chancy had come to get him. Of course she had. When he'd told her to keep his arrival secret he'd almost guaranteed that she'd be the one to pick him up.

He banked, lined up with the runway, dropped the flaps and coasted to a slow, smooth landing, as usual.

Giving her a quick wave, he secured the plane before grabbing his suitcase and laptop computer, then jogging over to join her.

"Any more problems?" was the first thing he said.

"Hello, to you, too," Chancy replied. "No. No more problems. It's almost been too quiet considering all that's happened lately."

"I know what you mean." He opened the van's passenger door and climbed in with his baggage while Chancy slid behind the wheel. "You can fill me in while we drive. You didn't tell my grandparents I was coming?"

"Nope. Not a peep. You asked me to keep it to myself and I did." She eyed him skeptically. "Why do you look surprised? I promised, didn't I?"

"Yes, but you're a woman. I never knew one who could keep a secret."

"Well, you do now."

"Apparently. Thanks for coming to pick me up."

She huffed and shot him a cynical look. "It's not like you gave me a lot of choice in the matter since no one else was supposed to know you were flying in. How long are you staying this time?"

He was getting the idea she wasn't too keen on him being there, which was illogical considering the fact that she'd been the one who'd phoned him in the first place. "I took a little vacation time. They won't call me to come back early unless the weather in tornado alley starts to fire up."

"Oh."

Not sure whether or not he should try further conversation, Nate fell silent. This was the first time he and Chancy had been together since she'd fled from him after the church service and there was a decidedly frosty atmosphere in the van. It was as if she were barely tolerating his presence. Oh, she was being polite enough. There was just something missing that they had shared before. Friendship? Camaraderie? All he knew was whatever had changed between them had altered their relationship on a level so basic it colored everything else.

"Tell me about the burglary at my grandparents' house," he finally said.

"There's not much to tell, really. Somebody waltzed in while Ted and Hester were at the grocery store and made off with the stack of pictures I had given her."

"The ones you got at the Hawkins auction?"

"Yes."

"Has it occurred to you that everything you and they have experienced can be tied to that auction?"

Chancy nodded. "Of course it has. I just can't see how a bunch of family photos can be that important to anyone but the family, themselves."

"I can't think of any other reason for all that's happened though, can you?"

"Unfortunately, no."

He took a deep breath and expelled it noisily, revealing his growing frustration. "There's also the possibility that this part of the country is finally catching up to the rest of the world."

"Meaning?" She was scowling at him.

"Meaning, the crime rate has always been low around here, or so the chamber of commerce has claimed. I wonder if that's still so."

"Don't be silly. Of course it is."

"It doesn't look like it to me."

"A couple of minor burglaries do not make a crime wave," Chancy argued. "Nothing was taken from my store and very little disappeared from Hester and Ted's."

"Don't forget the theft of this van," Nate said flatly.

"It was returned."

"That doesn't change the fact that it was taken in the first place." He paused, thoughtful. "You know, there might have been something valuable hidden in one of those photos you gave Grandma."

"Like what?"

"I don't know. Money? Stock certificates? Anything on paper could be slipped behind a picture without leaving any clue that it was there."

"That's true. If we still had the pictures we could look. I don't even know how many there were in the first place, do you?"

"No. The only time I handled them was when I moved them off this seat. There had to be at least ten or twelve."

"Well," Chancy said, "if we're right, we can all relax because the rash of burglaries should be over. The thief has the pictures."

"And if we're wrong?" Nate asked soberly. He saw her head snap around.

Her expression was determined and somber when she replied, "Then we'd all better start locking our doors."

Chancy pulled up to the front of the Collinses' house and left the van running while Nate got out with his suitcase. She was about to remind him to take his laptop, too, when she noticed that Domino wasn't standing guard the way he usually did.

She frowned. "That's odd."

"What is?"

"I don't see the dog."

"He's getting so deaf he probably didn't hear us drive up." Nate hoisted his bag and turned toward the house, calling, "Hey, Domino!"

Although she hadn't intended to tarry, Chancy was so uneasy she killed the engine and circled the van to catch up to him. "Wait a minute. I don't like the looks of this."

"Of what?" Nate asked. "Grandpa probably took the dog inside with him."

Chancy shook her head. "Uh-uh. It's after six-thirty. Ted and Hester must be at Wednesday-night church services. See? Their truck is gone."

"I hadn't noticed." Nate set his bag on the ground at his feet and studied the house. "You're right. Domino should be on the porch."

"And he isn't."

"I can see that."

"You don't have to get huffy. I just hope he's okay."

"Yeah, me, too," Nate said. "They've had that dog so long he's practically a member of the family."

"I think we should look for him before you go in, don't you?" She noted his skeptical expression to begin with, watched him reasoning it all out and recognized when he decided to concede.

"Okay," Nate said. "You go that way around the house and I'll go this way. I'll meet you in the barn. It's kind of cool tonight. He's probably napping on the straw in there because it's warmer."

Chancy arched an eyebrow but started off as Nate had suggested. She didn't believe for one second that the faithful old dog had abandoned his usual post just to take a comfortable nap in the barn. Animals were more predictable, more reliable, than people. When they felt they had an important assignment they seldom talked themselves out of doing their duty.

She rounded the corner of the old frame house and paused to peer beneath the drooping branches of a bridal veil spirea that was just finishing its spring bloom. Tiny white petals drifted down and caught in her hair as she brushed against the bush.

"Domino? Where are you, boy?"

Straightening, she dusted herself off and listened. Nothing stirred near the ground. A flock of purple martins was busy setting up housekeeping in the birdhouses Ted had erected between the house and barn, but other than that, all she could hear was Nate's voice in the distance, repeatedly calling the dog.

It was already getting dark. Soon, the only light in the yard would be from the full moon. An unexplainable sense of foreboding spurred her to hurry the rest of the way.

Nate was nearly to the barn when she turned the final corner and jogged up to him. "I didn't see any sign of him, did you?"

"No."

He peered into the barn through the open doorway. Chancy saw his eyes widen.

She followed his line of sight. "Oh, no!"

Nate was already headed for the dark shape lying so still on the floor. He bent over it and gently touched the fur. "Domino?"

"Is he…"

"He's still breathing," Nate said, "but it looks like he's been hurt."

"How badly?"

"I don't know. I can't tell. We need to get him to a vet."

"I agree. We'll use my van. Oh, poor Domino."

She watched Nate lift the dog gently and cradle him as best he could. Domino moaned, then raised his muzzle to try to lick Nate's face as if in gratitude.

Tears of sympathy filled Chancy's eyes. She blinked them back, praying they'd arrived in time to save the old dog's life.

It occurred to her that perhaps praying for an animal wasn't proper but she decided to do it anyway. If the good Lord didn't like the subject of her prayer, He could chalk it up to her human fallibility. She was sure it wouldn't be the first time—or the last—that she'd prayed in error, assuming that was the case in this instance.

Accompanying Nate, she tried to help him support Domino's head. The dog seemed to be drifting in and out of consciousness because sometimes it went limp all over.

"Lay him in the back," Chancy said.

"Right. I'll ride next to him so he won't be scared if he comes to."

She jerked open the door and held it while Nate carefully placed the dog on the floor and climbed in beside him. The sight of such a strong, capable man ministering to a helpless animal touched her deeply and made her further appreciate the tenderheartedness Nate was usually so careful to mask. In spite of everything, he was a truly kind man. One she had to admire.

As soon as he and the dog were settled, she slammed the back door, ran for the driver's seat and started the engine.

"It's too late for any animal hospitals to be open but one of the women in my Sunday-school class is a vet," Chancy called over her shoulder. "She lives on a ranch just down the road. Shall we take him there?"

"Whatever you think is best."

"Gotcha. Hang on!"

The man lurking inside the Collinses' farmhouse stood in the shadows and watched the animal rescue through the sheer lace curtains of an upstairs bedroom.

Stupid civilians. A person would think they'd have better sense than to take off like that without stopping to investigate how the dog had gotten hurt in the first place.

He chuckled wryly. *Too bad.* He'd have enjoyed

doing some damage to the people who had caused him so much trouble. Then again, their departure had provided more uninterrupted time in which to ransack the house, so he supposed it was for the best. Until he had recovered the lost keys he didn't want anyone to see him or be able to recognize him.

Glancing at the pocket watch he'd already stolen from the old man's dresser, he snorted cynically. It was getting late. There was no time to waste. The home owners would be back soon and he still hadn't searched the entire second story. If this job was going to be done right, he'd have to get a move on.

Later, after he had all the keys and had split the money in the lockers with his partners, he'd come back and settle the score.

By then it wouldn't matter if anybody saw him because they wouldn't live to tell about it.

Chancy raced her van down the long dirt driveway leading to the nearby Corbett ranch house.

Her friend Kara saw her coming and stepped out onto the porch as the tan vehicle slid to a stop in a similarly colored cloud of dust.

"Chancy! What's wrong?" Kara called.

She cranked down the window and leaned out. "I've got the Collinses' dog in the back. He's hurt."

"Let me see."

Chancy met her at the rear of the van and opened

the door. Nate was cradling Domino's head. The dog had regained consciousness and was panting rapidly.

"What happened?" the vet asked.

Nate straightened and eased out of the way to give her room to make an examination. "We don't know. We found him in the barn, out like a light. He came to but now he seems to be having trouble breathing."

"Probably broken ribs. I'll want X-rays," Kara said as she ran her hands over the dog's body from head to tail. "And there's a knot behind his ear with a fairly deep laceration, too. If I didn't know better, I'd say a horse had kicked him."

"My grandparents don't keep horses or cows anymore," Nate said.

"I know. Where were they when this happened?"

"Probably at church." Nate's worried gaze met Chancy's and held it.

She immediately understood. "I have my cell phone. I'll call the church to see if I can catch them there, then ask the sheriff to meet them at home, too, just in case."

"In case of what?" the vet asked.

Chancy hated to admit it but everything Nate had said earlier was true. "In case it's not safe. I don't care if Ted does get upset with me for asking for the sheriff's help. Whoever did this to Domino is not the kind of person I'd want two innocent folks like Hester and Ted to blunder into."

By the time Chancy and Nate were able to finish at the veterinarian's office and bring Domino home, it was almost 10:00 p.m. This time she drove more slowly to keep from jostling him, while Nate rode in the passenger's seat instead of lying on the floor with the old dog.

As they parked in front of the house, the older couple came out to meet them. Hester immediately hugged Nate while Ted followed Chancy to the rear of the van and watched her open the door to reveal the injured dog.

Domino's tail thumped against the floor at the sight of his master. Ted grinned. "Well, old boy, looks like you're gonna make it." His voice broke and he covered it by clearing his throat.

"Kara says he'll be sore for a while but he'll recover," Chancy told him. "She wrapped his ribs, put a couple of stitches in his head and gave him antibiotics to ward off infection."

"Poor old guy. Who would do such a thing?" Ted sounded incredulous.

"I don't know." Chancy looked at the house and noted lights shining in practically every window. "Did the sheriff come by to check the place out?"

"Yeah," Ted muttered. "Like a bull in a china shop. You should of seen the mess."

"Now, Ted," Hester interrupted, "that wasn't Harlan's fault and you know it. Look what happened to Nate's clothes."

"My clothes?"

"Yes," his grandmother explained. "Your suitcase was open and your clothes were spread all over the yard. I'm glad the sheriff let us know you were all right or I'd have been terribly worried about you, too."

Chancy stared at him, noting that he was doing the same to her. "You must have left your bag sitting outside when we went looking for Domino," she said. "Good thing you forgot your laptop in the van or it might have been ruined."

"Yeah. Evidently, whoever beat the dog decided to throw my stuff in the dirt. Nice neighborhood." He helped Ted lift Domino gently onto the ground. The dog was a bit unsteady but definitely happy to be home.

Hester paused to give Chancy a hug. "Bless your heart for helping us again," she said. "Would you like to come in and visit a spell? I can make tea."

"No. Thank you. I really have to be getting home." She caught Nate glowering at her. "And don't worry. I've changed all the locks on my doors since you were here last. My apartment is as secure as Fort Knox."

"Glad to hear it," he said flatly. "Good night."

"Good night. Don't forget your laptop," she said, handing it to him.

"Thanks."

"You're welcome. Good night again."

As she climbed back into the van and drove away she wondered if she was really as safe as she'd claimed. Thinking about what had happened to the innocent old dog made her skin crawl and her stomach knot. If the Collins family had been home they might have taken the brunt of the brutal attack, instead.

That idea, as unacceptable as it was, refused to go away. There *was* danger. And somehow, in spite of her blamelessness, she seemed to be an integral part of whatever was going on.

NINE

The next few days proved so uneventful Chancy began to think she'd been unnecessarily concerned. Either that or her conclusions about the stolen pictures had been correct and the threat was therefore over.

She knew she should have put those unsettling events behind her, yet she found her mind continuing to drift back to thoughts of Nate and the gentle way he'd cared for the injured dog. Apparently, all a man had to do to endear himself to her was to show kindness to helpless critters.

If he didn't insist on foolishly risking his own life all the time, maybe… She shook her head. *No. No way.* Nate might be perfect for some other woman but he was not acceptable in her book. As local fishermen liked to say when they caught the wrong species of fish, "This one's not a keeper. Throw him back." And that was exactly what she was doing, figuratively speaking, at least.

Chancy was puttering around the shop and congratulating herself for leading such a stable, rewarding life when the office phone rang. She caught it on the third ring. "Chancy's Second Chances. What can I do for y'all?"

"This is Nate Collins."

Heart leaping, she credited the reaction to a natural concern for his grandparents. "Are Hester and Ted okay?"

"They're fine."

That was a relief. "No more problems?"

"Thankfully, no. Listen, do you buy furniture in lots or by the piece?"

"Both. Why?"

"Because we have a houseful to sell and my grandmother wanted me to give you the option of being the first bidder."

Chancy's jaw dropped. "The whole household?"

"Yes. They're moving and they can't take it with them," he explained, sounding as if he assumed she'd have already known the answer.

"I thought you said they were fine."

"They are. They've finally seen the wisdom of moving to Oklahoma, that's all. Are you interested in the furniture or shall I call someone else?"

"No! Don't call anyone else. I'll be right over. Just give me a few minutes to lock up and put a note on the door."

"You need to hire somebody to keep your shop open while you're gone. Closing on a whim is ridiculous. It's bad for business."

"I can't really justify the extra expense. I never know when something like this will come up."

"Okay," Nate said. "Let's do it this way. I'll spend the day going through stuff with my grandparents and you can stop by after you close tonight. That'll give us a little more time to decide exactly what we're going to keep and what has to go."

"All right. See you about six-thirty?"

"That'll be fine."

Chancy bid him a polite goodbye and hung up quickly to keep from giving in to a strong desire to chastise him. As much as that stubborn man needed a good talking-to, she knew better than to argue with him more than she already had until she'd had a chance to visit with Hester and Ted and find out if moving away was what they truly wanted to do.

She'd often seen older people make emotional decisions when they were upset or confused and rue those decisions later. Once the Collins farm was sold and the household broken up there would be no going back, even if they changed their minds.

Chancy shook her head slowly, pensively. Ted and Hester had a lifetime of friends in Serenity. Their church family was here. Their history was here for generations back, too. The only tie they'd have to

Get 2 Books FREE!

Steeple Hill Books,
publisher of inspirational fiction, presents

Love Inspired
SUSPENSE

A SERIES OF EDGE-OF-YOUR-SEAT SUSPENSE NOVELS

FREE BOOKS!
Get two free books by acclaimed, inspirational authors!

FREE GIFTS!
Get two exciting surprise gifts absolutely free!

2 FREE BOOKS

▲ To get your 2 free books and 2 free gifts, affix this peel-off sticker to the reply card and mail it today!

GET 2 FREE BOOKS!

HURRY!

Return this card promptly to get **2 FREE Books** *and* **2 FREE Bonus Gifts!**

Love Inspired. SUSPENSE

YES! *Please send me the 2 FREE Love Inspired® Suspense books and 2 FREE gifts for which I qualify. I understand that I am under no obligation to purchase anything further, as explained on the back of this card.*

affix free books sticker here

323 IDL EL4Z   123 IDL EL3Z

FIRST NAME	LAST NAME

ADDRESS

APT.#	CITY

STATE/PROV.	ZIP/POSTAL CODE

Steeple Hill®

If offer card is missing write to: Steeple Hill Reader Service, 3010 Walden Ave., P.O. Box 1867, Buffalo, NY 14240-1867

BUSINESS REPLY MAIL
FIRST-CLASS MAIL   PERMIT NO. 717-003   BUFFALO, NY

POSTAGE WILL BE PAID BY ADDRESSEE

STEEPLE HILL READER SERVICE
3010 WALDEN AVE
PO BOX 1867
BUFFALO NY 14240-9952

NO POSTAGE
NECESSARY
IF MAILED
IN THE
UNITED STATES

Oklahoma was Nate, and thanks to his career choice, his future was anything but secure. The man chased tornadoes, for crying out loud. How long would he last if one of them caught *him,* instead of the other way around?

That vision of death and destruction gave her chills. She wrapped her arms around herself and shivered. He was going to be furious with her if she tried to talk some sense into his grandparents but she had to try. As their friend, she owed it to them.

And in the meantime, in case they were really dead set on moving, she'd run a trial balance in her checkbook and see how much she could afford to spend. Her fondest wish was that she wouldn't need a penny.

Chancy was watching the clock, nervously waiting for 6:00 p.m. so she could close her doors, when she heard the bell in the front of the shop jingle. Hoping it wasn't a customer who would dawdle for ages and then not buy, she hurried to greet the late arrivals and was surprised to see Louella Higgins in the company of Alice Franks and Joanna Jones, from Sunday-school class.

"Louella! Hello." She gave her mentor a hug, then smiled at the two women with her. "Welcome. What brings you all to my shop?"

"I was just passing by," Louella said, "and I saw these ladies outside so I told them all about your store and insisted they take a look." She turned to the round-faced, gray-haired woman and grinned. "See, Alice? I told you Chancy had lots of wonderful things for sale."

"That, she does. I'll have to come back when I have more time to shop. I wouldn't want to keep her after hours."

"Normally, I wouldn't mind a bit," Chancy said, "but tonight I have to go give an appraisal. Sorry."

That peaked Louella's interest. "Oh? Who's moving?"

"Nobody, I hope. I got a call from Nate Collins that Ted and Hester were thinking of selling out and leaving the state. I dearly wish they'd stay."

"Isn't that kind of sudden?"

"Not really. Nate has been trying to talk them into moving for ages. Maybe the burglary at their house convinced them."

"Maybe so. Well, I guess we'd better be going. Like Alice said, we don't want to make you late." Smiling, she turned to the younger woman. "Coming, Joanna?"

"I'll be right out. I just need to talk to Chancy for a second."

It was Joanna's obvious uneasiness that Chancy noticed most. The girl had clasped her hands together so tightly her knuckles were whitening and she seemed to be stalling until the others left. Unfortunately for Joanna, Louella and Alice dallied, too.

"Go ahead," Chancy urged her. "You're among friends."

"Well… Okay. I was wondering if you could use some part-time help. I don't know anything about antique furniture but I can learn. And I really need a job."

"I'm afraid—"

"Just give me a trial," the girl interjected pleadingly. "You won't even have to pay me at all if you don't like my work."

"Part-time, you say?"

"Yes. Any hours are fine. Honest. Then, even if you can't use me often I'll have a work record here and I can use you for references."

"I suppose that would be okay," Chancy said. She smiled benevolently and nodded, her mind made up. "The back room needs lots of cleaning up and sorting out. Come in on Friday and I'll give you an opportunity to show me what you can do."

"Super! Thanks."

Before the girl turned away, Chancy noted that there were unshed tears in her eyes. Poor thing. She must really need a job. Well, good. Now she had one, even if it wouldn't pay much. And the shop had the part-time help that Nate had insisted was needed.

She huffed in self-disgust. It was a relief to have someone lined up to substitute if she needed to go out. The only thing she didn't like about the arrangement was having to admit that Nate Collins had been right about anything.

Nate was waiting on the porch with Ted and Domino when Chancy pulled into the yard that evening. He was the only one who got up and came down the steps to greet her.

When she saw him glance at his watch she said, "Sorry if I'm a little late. Some people came in just as I was getting ready to close."

"Did they buy anything?"

Chancy smiled. "No. But I may have found that part-time employee you suggested. One of the women from my Sunday-school class stopped by to ask me for a job."

"Well, at least you know her."

"Yes, and no," Chancy said. "I only met her a couple of weeks ago."

"You didn't hire her, did you?"

She shrugged. "Sort of. I told her she could come in on Friday and I'd give her a trial. She doesn't know much about antiques but she's eager to learn. And she said she really needs the money, so…"

Nate was shaking his head. "I don't believe you people around here. You trust *everybody*."

"It's the way things are when you live in the country," Chancy replied. "You don't understand that because you're not…"

"From around here," he said to complete her sentence. "Yes, I know. And the longer I'm here, the happier I am that I'm not."

She squared her shoulders, her chin jutting with self-assurance and defiance. "That is the second saddest thing I've heard today."

"Oh?" His eyebrows arched. "What's the first?"

"That your grandparents are moving away. I think that's a huge, huge mistake."

"Opinion noted. And I'll thank you to keep it to yourself," Nate said matter-of-factly.

"In a pig's eye. You may think you have all the answers but you're not even close, mister." Continuing to face him, she fisted her hands on her hips. "Their whole life has been lived right here in Fulton County. What makes you think they'll be happy anywhere else?"

"People make adjustments all the time," Nate countered. "I've made arrangements for a retirement condo with all the amenities for them. They won't have to lift a finger."

"And that's your idea of doing a good deed? Get real. Do you think for one second that Ted will be happy sitting around all day long twiddling his thumbs or that Hester will want some maid or cook doing the chores she's handled all her life?"

"They've worked hard. They deserve an easy retirement."

"A path to feeling useless is more like it."

"Don't be ridiculous."

"You're the one being ridiculous, not me." Chancy stormed past him and headed toward the house.

Nate was right on her heels. "Hold it. You're not going to go in there and upset everybody."

"Oh, yeah? Watch me."

She felt his hand on her arm and jerked free of his grasp. Looking up, she saw Hester and Ted, standing together on the porch, observing the spirited conversation with fascination and a touch of amusement.

Nate apparently noticed his grandparents at the same time because he stopped trying to control Chancy.

She smiled and waved. "Hi! I was just on my way in to talk to you."

"No, she wasn't," Nate countered. "She isn't staying."

"Oh, yes, I am."

A giggle from the porch brought Chancy up short. Hester had her hand over her mouth to stifle her laughter but Ted wasn't even trying to mute his high spirits.

He guffawed and shook his head. "Listen to 'em, Mama. They sound just like we used to back when we was young, don't they?"

"Except that you were a tad more stubborn," Hester replied. "'Course, you were cuter, too. I always did have a soft place in my heart for those big blue eyes of yours."

"And there was none prettier than you," Ted told her with a tender smile and a peck on her cheek. "Still isn't."

"Thank you, dear." Hester grinned at her grandson. "If you two are through makin' a scene in the yard, what say we all go inside where we can talk like civilized folks?"

"Gladly." Chancy shot Nate the most tolerant look she could muster and walked away from him to lead the way. She knew he was following closely and looking daggers at her because the hair on the nape of her neck was prickling something fierce. Well, too bad. If he wanted to assert his supposed authority in regard to his extended family and they chose to take his advice, there was nothing she could do about it.

However, she didn't intend to stand by quietly while he talked those dear old people into making the biggest mistake of their lives. She'd seen it happen time and time again. A spouse would pass away or a person would get sick themselves and they'd be so overwrought and confused by the strain of the moment they'd make a snap decision, the kind of irreversible choice that they'd never have made under less stressful circumstances.

If she could prevent that sort of heartache in this case, she knew it was her duty to try.

Ted held the front door for Chancy and Hester to pass. Nate relieved him of it and gave him an affectionate pat on the shoulder. "Go on. Let's get this over with."

"You sound like a man with somethin' stuck in his craw." Ted chuckled. "Might as well get used to it, son. When a woman says she's right, you'd just as well agree with her. I learned a long time ago that there's no use arguing with 'em."

"That particular woman drives me crazy," Nate said quietly aside.

"So we noticed. The thing is, sometimes that can be a good sign."

"I don't see how."

"Maybe you will. Maybe not. That remains to be seen. Your grandma and I used to scrap a bit before we were married, too."

"Whoa." Nate stopped him by touching his arm. "Who said anything about marriage?"

"I thought I just did." The twinkle in Ted's eyes showed that he believed he was privy to a secret.

"Look," Nate said. "I'm not interested in getting married to *any* woman, especially not Chancy Boyd. She and I are totally wrong for each other. Period. End of story."

"Okay." The old man shrugged bony shoulders beneath his crisply ironed shirt. "If you say so."

"I do."

That innocent comment brought another spate of laughter from Ted.

"What's so funny?"

"Nothing much. With all this talk about gettin' married it sounded for a minute like you was practicin' your vows, that's all."

Nate huffed. It would be a long, cold day in July before he said *I do* to anyone, especially the young woman who was now seated on the sofa in the parlor bending his grandmother's ear with her negative opinions of the planned move. Chancy Boyd was a troublemaker with a chip on her shoulder the size of a bus.

He paused in the archway from the hall and studied her. Yes, she was attractive in a well scrubbed, natural way. And, yes, she was remarkable for both her accomplishments and her obvious intellect, but that was where his optimistic assessment ended.

Under other circumstances they might become friends, or perhaps even more, but as things stood, there was no way they could ever come to an understanding. His job was more than a living, it was his calling, just as some men were called to be teachers or pastors or even politicians.

What he did wasn't *work* in the sense of unwelcome toil done only for the money. Storm chasing was what gave his life value, made him who he was. He could never give it up, not even for love.

That conclusion brought Nate up short. *Love?* Except for one or two exceptions, his colleagues had clearly demonstrated the unlikelihood of finding a wife or girlfriend who would not only appreciate the importance of their endeavors but also lend emotional support. More than one supposedly stable marriage had broken up because of the traveling or the worry inherent in what he did. In Chancy's case, she was already overwrought about tornadoes. She'd never make it as his wife.

Did he wish it were not so? Nate asked himself. Gazing at her across the room he realized that, if he were totally honest with himself, he did wish they could become a couple. He also knew, without a shred of doubt, that there was not even the most remote chance of that happening.

"I got a part-time job at her store," Joanna told her husband. "I'll find out what happened to the collage real soon, now. I know I will. As soon as she leaves me alone I'll go through her stuff until I turn it up."

He paced the small apartment like a caged wild animal. "You'd better. If I don't get back to Little Rock by tomorrow—with those keys—my partners are coming here. They're mad as hornets."

She shivered. "I'm so sorry. I was positive it had to be in that house. That's where the other pictures from the auction ended up."

"Well, it wasn't. I turned that place upside down and inside out."

"I know. I heard that the people who live there got so scared they're thinking of moving away."

"You'd better hope they don't go anywhere till we get my keys back," he warned. "If they try to leave I'll do whatever I have to do to stop them." He glared at her. "Got that?"

She merely nodded. She knew all too well what he was capable of and she didn't want to see anyone hurt.

At Chancy's urging, Ted and Nate had gone out to the barn to make a list of the farm equipment that would have to be sold, leaving the women alone in the house.

Chancy took advantage of the temporary privacy. "All I ask is that you sleep on it for a week or so, Hester, and think it through. Remember, once you sell everything and leave here, you'll never be able to afford to come back."

"We can visit," the older woman said.

"Of course you can. And we'd certainly want you to. I just worry that you'll change your mind once you've moved. I can think of several old friends who left here not too long ago and wish they hadn't."

"You mean like Wanda and Charity?"

"Among others. They liquidated everything of value and when they found out it cost more than they'd thought it would to live somewhere else, they ended up in a bind."

"We have Nate," Hester said. "He'll look after us."

"As long as he's around, I'm sure he will," Chancy replied. "The thing is, he's not only away from home a lot, he's in a dangerous profession. What if something happened to him? What would you and Ted do then?"

"I don't know. I suppose it would be wise to find out how much that fancy condo costs in case we do have to take over and pay for everything ourselves."

"I'd certainly ask questions like that before I pulled up stakes and made a permanent move. And I'd want to look the new place over, too. I mean, what if you don't care for it?"

"I would like to figure out how much of my furniture I can take." Hester let her gaze drift over her assembled possessions, pausing briefly on this and that. "The sideboard over there belonged to my mama. She was so proud when Papa gave it to her. He cut trees and skidded logs all one spring just to save up the money. And that pretty pink glass basket was my grandma's. There's a note inside that says she got it for a wedding present."

"Those things are irreplaceable," Chancy said, patting the older woman's hands. "You know that."

"I know."

"Then you will think about it?"

"Yes." Her shoulders slumped. "I don't really want to move away but this old place is gettin' to be a lot of work for Ted to take care of. I want to do what's best for him."

"I know you do. Tell you what." Chancy brightened and smiled. "I'll make a list of the larger items, like the antique sideboard and the other furniture, then take the list back to my shop and do some research so I can give you firm prices. How does that sound?"

"How long will all that take?" Hester asked with a raised eyebrow and a mischievous grin.

Chancy laughed lightly. There was clearly no moss growing on Hester Collins's brain. "As long as you want it to, Miss Hester. Just as long as you want it to."

Hester chuckled. "That's what I was hopin' you'd say."

TEN

Chancy was still making a detailed list of the Collinses' household contents and smiling over Hester's clever suggestion to delay the whole process when the men returned from the barn.

She glanced briefly at Nate and caught him glowering at her. "This is going to take me hours, maybe days," she said brightly. "It's amazing how many wonderful items are crammed into this little farmhouse."

"The yard and the barn are full, too," Nate grumbled. "Looks like we'll have to arrange an auction like the one they had at the Hawkins place. I can't see any other way to dispose of everything and still get fair prices."

"I promised Hester I'd give her firm bids on some special items in the house," Chancy said. "When I get my list done I'll know more."

"Can't you give us a ballpark figure?"

"Not without taking the chance I'll inadvertently

cheat you," she replied sweetly. "I certainly wouldn't want to offer too little."

His eyebrow arched and he stared at her. "How long will that take?"

"Hester asked me the same thing. I'll do my best but I may have to do some extensive research on the Internet before I'm sure."

"That's ridiculous. You deal in antiques all the time. You must know approximately what they're worth."

"Yes, and no. There are some really rare items here."

"Then I can assume you'll be offering high dollar?"

She winced, hoping the reaction didn't show. The man was as quick-witted as his grandmother. Clearly, he already suspected a delaying tactic and wasn't about to sit still for it. Well, so what? She'd promised Hester that she'd stall and that was exactly what she intended to do.

To Chancy's relief the older woman came to her rescue by changing the subject.

"I want to give a lot of the smaller things that I don't need to the church rummage sale," Hester said. "Ted and I already took a whole boxful in when we went to services last Wednesday evening." Her cheeks reddened. "Oh, dear. I just thought of something. That little picture you gave me, with the photographs from Jewel and Pete's, was in that batch of stuff. I'm sorry. I should have offered it back to you instead."

"No problem," Chancy said. "I can always buy it

at the rummage sale if I really want it. That way the proceeds will go to support the church."

"Well, I'm still sorry," Hester insisted. "I loved it but like I told you before, Ted wasn't keen on hangin' it on the wall. I never thought about it when I stuffed it in with the giveaways."

"No problem. Speaking of your being gone last Wednesday night," Chancy said, "how's Domino doing? I noticed he was lying on the porch but he didn't get up to greet me the way he usually does."

"He's still a little stove-in," Ted said. "Kinda like me. We both get around okay, though."

"Glad to hear it." Chancy noted the somber, concerned expression on Nate's face when he looked at his grandfather. She knew his interference wasn't malicious but that didn't mean he was doing the right thing. "Maybe we should take you to the vet, too," she teased Ted.

"Be better'n most doctors, I reckon," Ted said with a grin. "I'm not keen on modern medicine. My grandpa ate fried taters and red-eye gravy every day of his life and it finally killed him, just like the experts said it would—at the age of ninety-two."

Chancy laughed. "I don't doubt it. Folks in those days stayed active because they had to, instead of being couch potatoes, and I think it was the best thing for them." She eyed Nate. "Sometimes, being idle is *not* wise."

"Neither is working yourself to death or falling off a roof because you had to climb up there to fix it."

Chancy shook her head. "You are one stubborn man. You know that?"

Nate scowled at her, much to Ted and Hester's amusement. "I wouldn't be surprised to see *your* picture in the dictionary next to the word *stubborn.*"

"Then yours will be next to the definition of a mule. And don't look at me like that. You started this."

Nate set his jaw. "Just remember, Ms. Boyd. I never give up, especially when I know I'm right, so when you're making your estimates on the furniture, don't make the mistake of underestimating *me.*"

"I don't think there's any chance of that," she said. "I know exactly what I'm up against." *And you don't scare me.*

She meant that thought with all her heart, yet in the deepest reaches of her subconscious there was fear, not *of* Nate but *for* him. Although they were at odds over his grandparents' future, she could tell that he cared deeply for them and they clearly loved him, too. According to local gossip, their own son, Nate's father, had long been alienated from them. If something bad happened to Nate, the trauma of losing him would kill them. Didn't he see that? Didn't he care?

Chancy sighed and refocused on the task at hand. She really did intend to give Hester fair bids on the furniture, although most of it wasn't very valuable. The pink glass basket that had been Hester's grandmother's was probably early Fostoria and the Eastlake-style sideboard looked handmade in spite of the fact that factories had been producing similar pieces by the late 1890s. Of all the antiques and collectibles in the Collins house, it was likely that Hester would decide to keep those two items, so their higher value was a moot point, anyway.

Sadly, most of the other stuff belonged in the church rummage sale with the things Hester had already given away, Chancy concluded. She'd go through the things upstairs and in the attic but she doubted she'd find more than a dozen or so additional items that were worth buying for her shop. The true value was in the memories, the history. There were always special trinkets that brought back fond remembrances and should be retained.

In her case, however, the destruction of the family home had resulted in no important material loss. There was nothing from her childhood that she wanted to remember. If she hadn't turned to God in her teens, as a last resort, she didn't know how she could have coped with the demoralizing atmosphere in the house where she'd grown up.

Yes, she missed her parents in spite of the fact that they'd used her as a means to try to get back at each other. She'd been the proverbial "rope" in their cruel game of emotional tug-of-war and she couldn't help being thankful that the terrible game was finally over.

Did that make her a bad person? She didn't think so. She'd discussed that disturbing question with Pastor Malloy and he had wisely asked her if she believed God would be unfair to any of His children simply because she'd prayed for her own release.

The answer was *no,* of course. Still, it continued to bother her that she hadn't listened to the whispers in her subconscious to go to see her parents that fateful day.

That realization had left her more aware of other people's feelings, made her more empathetic to their plights. Now, when the Lord laid a concern on her heart, she acted as best she could and as quickly as she was able, whether it was a phone call to check someone's welfare or a hot meal delivered to a shut-in or merely a prayer for their well-being.

Which reminded her, the whole Collins family was still in need of some serious prayer.

She smiled slightly and thought of Nate as she started upstairs to continue her survey.

While she was at it, she'd better include herself in those prayers and ask for more forbearance, she decided, because as long as that man was around she was going to need all the extra patience she could muster.

* * *

"Friday, I'm supposed to go through a whole stack of boxes and junk in the back room and sort it out. I'm bound to find my missing collage then."

"I told you I can't give you that much extra time," he said, scowling. "Get it—or I'm taking over."

"What can you do that I can't?"

His laugh was sinister, coarse. "I can *make* her tell me where it is, that's what."

"Oh, Sam, you wouldn't hurt her, would you? I mean, she hasn't done anything to us. Not on purpose. And she seems like a really nice lady."

He snorted cynically. "Good. The nice ones cave in easier. I kind of hope you don't find the rest of the keys. I think I'd enjoy making your new boss talk."

Joanna gripped his forearm and felt his muscles tense beneath her fingers. It wasn't normal for her to stand up to him but this time she knew she had to. "Don't you touch her, you hear? She's the first person who's been good to me in longer than I can remember."

One side of his mouth lifted in a sneer. "Oh, yeah? What about me, darlin'? Did you forget your lovin' husband?"

"No, Sam, I didn't forget you. I couldn't. I wouldn't. But you've been away a long time and I've been moving around so much I didn't make friends. Not real ones. But Chancy's different. She likes me. She really likes me. I can tell. And I like her, too."

"Then you'd better go to work and find those keys," he warned, "or your wonderful boss is going to wish you had."

Chancy's new employee was waiting for her outside the front door when she went downstairs to open the shop the following morning.

"Joanna! This is a surprise."

"I was too excited to wait," the girl said. "You don't have to pay me for today. You can just show me around and stuff, okay?"

"Okay," Chancy said, ushering her in and changing the hanging sign on the door from Closed to Open.

"I didn't see you drive up," Joanna said. "Did you park out back?"

"No. I live right here." She pointed to the hidden door that stood ajar. "See how that bookcase swings out? It's really the entrance to my upstairs apartment."

"Wow. Cool. Like a secret passage, huh?"

"I guess you could say that. It's very handy sometimes, especially in bad weather."

"Right. You won't get rained on going home."

Chancy was amused by the young woman's interest. "Come on. I'll show you the office and give you a safe place to stash your purse, then we'll take the grand tour."

"I don't know much about antique furniture, like

I said, but I know I can learn." Joanna tugged the hem of her black T-shirt into place over her denim-clad hips. "I hope this outfit is good enough. I noticed you were wearing jeans when I was here before so I figured it was okay."

"It's fine. You need something durable and casual when you're moving or sorting things in the back room. It gets pretty dusty back there."

"You sure have a lot of stuff."

"Too much," Chancy said amiably. "I tend to get a little carried away when I go to big sales and auctions."

"I thought I'd seen you before we met in church. I guess it must have been at an auction."

"Do you go to a lot of them? I usually remember people I run into on a regular basis and I can't say your face was familiar."

"I haven't lived in Serenity for very long."

"Well, you're going to love it here," Chancy said with a smile. "And our Sunday-school class is amazing. Those women can be closer than sisters once you get to know them." She paused and studied her new employee's suddenly pained expression. "Do you have family nearby?"

"No," Joanna said flatly. "I don't have anybody."

Giving her a brief hug and a smile, Chancy told her, "Well, you do now. Welcome to Serenity. We're like one big family. Like I said, you're going to love it here."

* * *

Nate didn't want to visit Chancy's Second Chances but he'd gotten no satisfaction when he'd phoned her so he decided he should talk to her in person.

The waiflike young woman who greeted him in the front of the store was definitely no one he knew. "Hi." He peered past her. "Is Chancy here?"

"In the back," the girl said. "We were cleaning up. Can I help you?"

"I doubt it, but thanks." Nate started past her and noted that she jumped back as if she were leery of letting him get too close. That reaction made him assess his approach to see if he'd been acting overly brusque. He decided he hadn't been, at least, no more than usual. Chancy had certainly never seemed cowed by his forthright manner.

He found her sitting on a spindly stool in the midst of piles of dusty, tattered cardboard boxes. "I thought you were working on the estimate for my grandparents," he said.

"I was. I am. I've put out some feelers and I'm waiting to get e-mails back from larger auction houses."

"You mean like Sotheby's or Christie's?"

"Not *that* big." Chancy giggled. "I was thinking more of a few places in Little Rock or Memphis. You know, big cities that are still fairly close by."

He eyed the littered storeroom. "What are you doing while you wait?"

"Charity work. We're sorting out a lot of this stuff that's not suitable for the shop so we can give it to Serenity Chapel for their rummage sale."

"Which reminds me," Nate said. "Grandma's still fretting about that picture of yours that she gave them. I told her to just go ask for it back but she says she's too embarrassed. Maybe, when you take all this over there, you could take a look at it and tell her you hate it, assuming you do. If not, I imagine they wouldn't mind putting it aside for you."

"I think she's making a mountain out of a mole-hill," Chancy said with a tender smile. "I don't even remember what it looked like."

"The way she described it, it's junk jewelry stuck to a background in some kind of funny design. She said it wasn't very big." He held his hands parallel to indicate a span of eight or nine inches. "Maybe like so."

"Okay. I'll take a peek if it'll make her feel better. It doesn't sound like anything I could sell in here unless some of the jewelry is antique and, even then, it was probably ruined when it was glued down."

"Beats me," Nate said. He scanned the assembled clutter. "Well, I guess I'll go and leave you to your work. Looks to me like you've got a long day ahead of you."

"A long several days but we'll get a handle on it pretty soon, especially since I have help now."

Chancy looked past him, expecting to see her new employee lingering in the background. "That's funny."

"What is?"

"Joanna. I thought she was right here. Did you see her when you came in?"

"A thin girl with long brown hair and a scarf on her head? Yeah. She offered to help me. She's probably out in the front waiting on somebody else."

Chancy got to her feet and dusted off her jeans. "I don't think so. She hasn't been trained for that. Besides, I didn't hear the bell."

As she brushed past Nate she explained, "I had to rig a bell on the front door so I'd hear if anyone came in while I was working in the back. I might have overlooked its chimes because I was talking to you, but I don't think so."

He followed her through the connecting door to the sales rooms of her shop and into the small office near the cash register.

Chancy's eyes were wide when she turned to face him. "That's odd. Her purse is gone. She showed up early even though I'd told her not to come in till Friday, so why would she suddenly leave without saying a word?"

"Maybe she quit."

"After begging me for this job?"

"You'd better check the till," Nate cautioned,

frowning and scanning the tiny office. "Do you know how much cash you had on hand?"

"Of course I do. But Joanna wouldn't rob me. She's a sweet little thing."

"She struck me as awfully jumpy," Nate said. "Maybe she was casing the place all along."

"I don't believe that for a second." Chancy opened the cash register and did a quick count. "Looks to me like it's all here. I have more money locked in an old safe in the back room but I didn't give her the combination so she couldn't have touched that." Shooting him an I-told-you-so look, she added, "Your imagination is working overtime again."

"Maybe, but it seems to me she'd have had to work at it to slip out without ringing your bell."

Nate continued to assess the peaceful antique store as he headed for the door himself. "Remember what they say, 'Just because you're paranoid doesn't mean no one is out to get you.'"

"Well, that's certainly not a very comforting thought."

He paused with his hand on the knob and raised an eyebrow. "It wasn't meant to be."

ELEVEN

As soon as Nate left, Chancy used the phone number she had for her new employee and tried to contact her. All she got for her trouble was a recorded message that the cell-phone user was unavailable.

She tried three more times during the afternoon, without success, before she decided to visit the young woman in person as soon as she closed the shop that evening.

Planning that visit, she realized belatedly that she had failed to ask for a home address, Social Security number or any other official ID. Nate was right. She'd been terribly lax. Since Joanna had arrived before she was expected and Chancy had never hired anyone before, it hadn't occurred to her that she'd need more personal information up front.

Racking her brain for what to do next, she remembered the contact slip Louella always asked newcomers to fill out when they first visited her

Sunday-school class. Not only would the teacher probably have an address to go with Joanna's phone number, Chancy thought it would be good to talk to someone else about her confusing feelings regarding Nate Collins. No one was more wise, understanding and empathetic than Louella Higgins.

Chancy found her teacher and mentor tending a freshly tilled garden plot behind the house.

Louella straightened, dusted off her hands and smiled. "Well, lookie who's here! You're just in time to help me get the rest of these tomato plants in the ground before dark." She eyed the cloudy sky. "Looks like it's fixin' to rain so they'll get watered good, too."

"Gladly."

Chancy stuffed her keys into her purse, laid it to one side on the grass and picked up a trowel. "Isn't it a bit early in the year, though? Aren't you afraid we'll have a late freeze?"

"Nope. I heard the whip-poor-will sing last night so we know he's gettin' ready to nest. That always means the coldest nights are over."

"I'd forgotten about that old saying. Are you sure the bird knows best?" Chancy asked.

"Never has failed me in the past." Louella handed her a plastic tray containing a half dozen spindly plants. "Bury 'em real deep so all that's above ground is the very top leaves. That way they'll make more roots from the stem."

"Yes, ma'am." She eyed what her friend had already done, copied the spacing between plants, dropped to her knees and went to work. "I stopped by to ask you a favor," she said as she dug.

"Sure. What can I do for you?"

"Remember when you and Alice were at my shop and I told Joanna Jones I'd give her a job?"

"Sure, I remember. Why?"

Chancy sat back on her heels. "Well, I need to get in touch with her but I didn't ask her for enough personal information right away. She's not answering her cell phone and I can't find her listed in the phone book or on the Internet. I wondered if you might have her home address from class."

"Most likely." Louella frowned at her across the garden plot. "Is there a problem?"

"I don't really know. She seemed to be doing fine until this afternoon when she just walked out of the shop without a word to me."

"That's odd."

"I know. She was there when Nate Collins stopped by to talk to me about Hester and Ted. When we looked for her after that, she was gone."

"Nate Collins, you say? Well, well." Louella had begun to grin.

"Yes, and don't look at me like that. He and I have absolutely nothing in common."

"Oh, I don't know. You both seem real fond of his grandparents."

"That's another drawback. Nate keeps trying to talk them into selling out and moving to Oklahoma. I've promised Hester I'd stall before making estimates on their furniture to give her and Ted time to think things over, but Nate keeps pressing me for answers."

"Maybe he just wants an excuse to keep seeing you."

"I doubt that very much. He usually sounds as if he's mad at me."

"Or mad at himself for liking you?"

Chancy's head snapped up and she stared at her friend. "I hadn't thought of it quite that way." Mulling over the situation, she shook her head. "No. It can't be that. He was nicer to me when we barely knew each other."

"Okay. Whatever you say. Still, he did come to church for the first time in who-knows-how-long. And he did sit by you, in case you've forgotten."

"I'm not likely to forget that morning," Chancy said flatly. "That was when I found out he chases tornadoes for the National Weather Service. On purpose. What kind of fool does that?"

"Humph. He's a man. They have too much bravery hardwired into their little brains. They can't help it."

"Well, it can help getting involved with him," Chancy replied. "I'm already worried enough because of his grandparents. I'm not going to have anything more to do with him than I absolutely have to."

"Then you've decided to tell him you aren't interested in Hester's furniture?"

"Well, no, but…"

"Aha! I thought so. Face it, girl. If you weren't the tiniest bit anxious to spend more time with Nate you'd have told him to buzz off long ago and to take his family's furniture with him."

Chancy made a wry face. Louella was right. She'd had every opportunity to tell Nate she wasn't interested, yet doing so had never occurred to her until Louella had mentioned the possibility. Could she really, subconsciously, want to be around him? Was she that far gone? She hadn't thought so until now.

Picturing his face, thinking about seeing him again, she felt a sudden rush of excitement, of joy. *Uh-oh.* That was not a good sign. Definitely not. Was Louella right? Was she stringing Nate along because of ulterior motives that she herself hadn't acknowledged until now?

Oh, dear God, I hope not, she prayed silently. *I've already lost my whole family to a tornado. Please, please, please, don't let me fall in love with that man!*

The address Louella had given Chancy led her to a run-down apartment complex on the outskirts of town. The so-called lawn was overgrown, the paint was peeling and there was a rusty, dented blue car parked in the unpaved driveway. Observation would have led her to believe the place was abandoned if she hadn't known otherwise.

Chancy found the number she was looking for and rapped on the door.

She was about to repeat the knock when Joanna opened the door and peeked out.

The girl's eyes widened in astonishment. Her jaw gaped. "What are *you* doing here?"

"I was worried about you," Chancy explained. "Are you all right?"

The girl slipped outside without fully opening the door and drew it quietly closed behind her. "I'm fine."

"You left so quickly this afternoon I was worried."

"I said I'm fine." Gusty wind was ruffling her long hair and she tossed it back, away from her face.

"Okay. Shall I expect you back at work tomorrow?"

"No."

"I'm sorry to hear that." Overlapping the front of her pale blue nylon jacket, Chancy held it tightly to her to ward off the evening chill. "Was it something I said or did?"

"No. I just quit, okay?"

"Okay." Chancy saw tears filling the young woman's eyes and watched her fighting to temper her emotions. "I feel I owe you a little in wages. If you'll stop by the store I'll write you a check."

"Yeah, sure. Maybe in a few days."

"Will I see you in church this Sunday?"

Joanna shook her head and lowered her gaze so that her long, dark hair fell against her cheeks and partially hid her expression as she said softly, "I don't think so."

Touched, Chancy gave her shoulder a brief pat, then stepped away. "All right. Just remember you're always welcome at Serenity Chapel, no matter what."

When the girl whispered, "I don't think so," again, tears began to slide down her cheeks.

"Well, *I* do. Remember what Jesus said about having to be sinless to qualify to cast the first stone? None of us is that perfect. Far from it."

"You don't know me."

"No, but I'd like to," Chancy said. "Why don't we go get a cup of coffee or an ice cream and talk this over? My treat." She noticed the cautious, almost fearful glance the girl cast over her shoulder toward the apartment.

"I can't."

"Well, maybe some other time. I could stop by again."

"No! Don't do that. Don't ever do that, you hear?"

Frowning, Chancy backed away. "Okay. I won't. Sorry I bothered you."

There was something wary and fearful about the girl's expression, something that reminded Chancy of a trapped animal that was casting around for any means of escape.

She had noticed an uneasiness in both of the younger new members of the Sunday-school class when she'd first met them but this reaction was far beyond mere nervousness or social anxiety.

Well, she thought sighing, *if she won't talk to me or let me help, there's really nothing more I can do.*

With a wave and a nod she turned and headed for her van. Whatever the problem was, it was clear that this young woman could use a lot of prayer.

That obvious conclusion made Chancy smile as she climbed into the van and drove away. There wasn't a single person in the world who couldn't use more prayer, was there? Herself included.

The pounding on the rear door of the shop below caught Chancy's attention in spite of the ten o'clock news she was watching on television. Who in the world was making all that racket? They sounded frantic!

Frowning, she peered out her upstairs window and saw Ted Collins's pickup truck parked in the glow of the streetlight next to her van.

Her heart jumped and began to race. Something must be terribly wrong for Nate or his grandfather to be hammering on her door this late!

Instead of taking the time to go through the shop and

unlock everything, she left her apartment by the back door and hurried down the wooden exterior stairway.

Her visitor spotted her, stopped banging on the warehouse door and quickly joined her.

"Nate? What's wrong? Has something happened to Hester or Ted?" The frigid night winds made Chancy wish she'd stopped to grab her jacket. She shivered.

"No. They're fine."

"Then what…" She could see the telltale creases in his forehead, the hard set of his mouth. Whatever was bothering him had to be dire.

"The crime wave in your peaceful little town isn't over, after all," he said flatly. "We just got word the church was vandalized tonight."

"Serenity Chapel? You can't be serious!"

"Oh, I'm more than serious," he answered. "One of my grandmother's friends called a few minutes ago and told her all about it."

"But, why did you come here and raise such a ruckus? If you wanted me to know, why not phone?"

"Because I needed to see for myself that you were okay." His scowl deepened. "I think I've finally figured out what's been going on."

Chancy rolled her eyes. "Well, I sure wish you'd let me in on it. I have no idea."

"You would if you'd put the clues together logically the way I did." He eyed the dark antique store before his gaze traveled to the windows of her well-lit apartment above. "Get in the truck. We'll talk while we drive to the church."

"What?"

"This all revolves around you, Chancy. I didn't make the complete connection until the church burglary but I thought about it all the way over here and everything makes sense now."

"To you, maybe." Hands fisted on her hips, she faced him. "I'm not going anywhere with you unless you tell me what's going on."

"It's not about those old photographs from the Hawkins auction, the way we'd thought before," he said. "It's about that picture you gave my grandmother. It has to be. I don't know whether it's the jewelry in it that's valuable or if there's something else hidden in the frame, but when you concentrate on that particular item, all the crimes tie together."

Her jaw dropped and her eyes widened. "That useless little thing?"

"Apparently." He slipped his arm around her shoulders to warm her, protect her and guide her. "Come on. The burglar was interrupted before he could go through the entire rummage-sale collection. If we're lucky we may find that the picture is still there."

"I have to get a coat and my purse," she said, resisting his urging.

"I'll come up with you. I'm not letting you out of my sight."

"Don't be silly. I'm fine. So is my apartment. The only disturbance around here tonight was when you started banging on my door."

"As far as you know it was, but that may not be the actual case," Nate countered. "I won't be satisfied until we get to the bottom of this."

"Okay. Follow me." Embarrassed, she gave him a lopsided smile. "Just wait for me out on the landing, will you? I imagine half the gossips in this part of town are peeking out their windows at us right now."

He cast a furtive glance from side to side as he said, "The only person I'm worried about is the guy who was seen running from the church."

"They're sure it was a man?" Chancy asked as they climbed the stairs.

"That's what the rumor mill says. Supposedly a big, burly guy."

"Good." She paused at her door and turned to him. "Because my first thought was to blame Joanna and there's no way she could ever be mistaken for a muscular man."

The slicker-clad sheriff was lounging against his patrol car, talking to the church pastor, when Nate and Chancy arrived at Serenity Chapel. He touched the brim of his Smokey Bear hat and grinned. "Evening, folks. Come to see the show?"

Nate gave him a stony look. "We came to help, Sheriff."

"Yes," Chancy said, "We think we've figured out what's been going on, including the break-in at the Collins farm."

"You don't say."

"We do say." She smiled at Logan Malloy. "Good evening, Brother Logan."

Logan returned her smile. "Evening. Mind if I listen to your theory, too?"

"No. Not at all," Nate answered. He eyed the sky where distant lightning was illuminating the clouds like the flame from a hundred flickering candles. "But let's go inside before we get rained on. If we can locate a picture that was in with a donation my grandmother made, we may be able to tie up all the loose ends at once."

Leading the way, Logan shook his head as he said, "That promises to be a pretty big job, considering what happened in here tonight. Some of our folks are trying to put it right but it's an enormous job, as you'll see." He opened the door to the auditorium in the rear of the building and stood back. "Have a look."

Chancy gasped. "Oh, my!"

Long, rectangular tables that had been piled high with goods for the upcoming rummage sale were swept clean and the aisles between them were littered with mounds of clothing, trinkets and who-knows-what. In spite of the ongoing efforts of several familiar women, including Louella and Alice, the mess was still extensive.

"This is awful!" Chancy exclaimed.

"It's also helpful." Nate passed her and made his way through the room by skirting the workers and the debris. "We can see exactly where the ransacking stopped. Therefore, the burglar either found what he was looking for and quit or was interrupted before he was finished. Either way, we only have to search the areas he didn't touch."

"That's right!" She smiled appreciatively. "How did you get so smart?"

"All you need to do is reason logically," Nate answered.

"And I don't?"

"I didn't say that." He raised and eyebrow and gave her a cynical look. "However…"

"Never mind. You're right. I am too apt to jump to easy conclusions instead of looking for less obvious answers to puzzles."

Like what am I going to do about my feelings for you? she added to herself, then said, "Okay. The picture we want is eight or nine inches square, give or take a few inches." She held out her hands to demonstrate to everyone present. "And it has old jewelry glued to it. That's really all I know but it should be enough to go on. There can't be many like it."

"Which means it was probably handmade," Nate said slowly, thoughtfully. "Do you have any idea who the artist might be?"

"I don't." Chancy scanned from the pastor to the other women and then the sheriff. "Do any of you?"

They all shook their heads, so she went on. "Okay then. Let's dig in. You each take an aisle on that side of the room and Nate and I will search over here." She felt her cheeks warm as she realized she'd been giving orders and looked to Nate. "If that's all right with you."

"No problem," he said seriously. "The sooner we find the picture, the sooner we can relax."

"Maybe we should call in some more of the women who were working on setting up this sale and see if they noticed it or know where it was put," Logan Malloy suggested.

Chancy shook her head. "I don't want to bother anybody else this late at night. If we don't find it there'll be plenty of time to ask for extra help later."

As everyone set to work picking through the boxes and bags of donated items, Chancy began to mull over Nate's conclusions. His hypothesis did seem to fit. The first sign of trouble had been right after the auction and it was obvious that the contents of her van had been rifled. So had the pile of boxes she'd temporarily left behind.

And what had she bought that hadn't ended up

either place? Only the stack of pictures that she'd given to Hester almost immediately.

Her heart began to pound, her hands tremble. She racked her brain, trying to recall minute details involving the days since then. Who else knew about her gift to Hester? Had she mentioned it to very many people?

A replay of her conversation with Louella Higgins after church popped into her mind. The dispersal of the pictures hadn't been a secret so there was no reason to think that Louella had kept it to herself. Or that Hester had. Literally dozens of people probably knew the whole story by now.

Plus, there was the matter of Joanna Jones. Chancy worried her bottom lip with her teeth. Joanna had shown up looking for work at precisely the opportune time, hadn't she? And she'd walked out right after Nate had mentioned that the picture was still at the church, awaiting resale.

Chancy sighed. As much as she hated to admit it, she might have misjudged the young woman, might have trusted her too fully. Though she hadn't been the one seen fleeing after the church break-in, she might somehow be connected to the whole intrigue. The idea was certainly plausible.

The signs of fright Joanna had displayed were beginning to make sense, too. If there was another person involved, and if that person was the man who'd been spotted fleeing from this auditorium, it was no wonder the poor girl had acted so afraid. Whatever her connection might be, a frail woman like Joanna was no match for a muscular man with crime on his mind.

Chancy paused and glanced at the sheriff, noting that he wasn't working nearly as hard as the rest of them were. "Harlan? I know you're supposed to be off duty for the night already, but would you mind checking on somebody's welfare for me? It's on your way."

"S'pose not. Who needs to be looked after?"

"A girl who used to work for me. She didn't last long and I got the feeling there may have been more going on in her life than she let on." Straightening, Chancy reached into her pocket and retrieved a crumpled scrap of paper. "She lives in those apartments by the river on Highway 9. The ones right off the access road to the boat-launching ramp. Know where I mean?"

"Sure. There's a big turnover in that place. What's her name?"

"Joanna Jones," Chancy said, handing him the scrap of paper. "This is her apartment number. When I stopped by there to ask her why she'd quit, she acted awfully nervous, as if she didn't want me around. I didn't think much about it at the time but now I wonder if there was somebody else with her in the apartment. Somebody she didn't want me to know about."

"Sure, I'll take a look," the lawman said as he hefted his gun belt and squared his beefy shoulders. "I should be gettin' home, anyways, 'fore my wife forgets what I look like."

"Just be careful, okay? And if there is a problem, tell Joanna I meant what I said about the Lord taking care of His own. If she needs help, all she has to do is ask the folks in this church and we'll be there for her. Remind her?"

"Will do." Harlan touched the brim of his hat and nodded before he turned to leave. "'Night all."

"'Night, Sheriff," Chancy said. "And thanks."

"Just doin' my job."

She heard a huff behind her and glanced at Nate. He was rolling his eyes and arching his dark eyebrows as if he seriously doubted the other man's diligence.

Truth to tell, she'd have felt better about the whole situation if she could have accompanied Harlan to the girl's apartment and seen for herself that everything was all right, even if it was probably unwise to do so.

A shiver skittered up Chancy's spine and prickled the fine hairs at her nape. She didn't like feeling afraid and she wasn't sure how to eliminate the constant insistence of her subconscious that she was getting deeper and deeper into trouble—trouble she couldn't see and therefore couldn't avoid.

One thing I can do, she told herself with decisiveness. *I can stop having anything to do with Nate Collins.*

She inhaled deeply and released it as a sigh. *Yeah, right. That stupid plan didn't work before and it's not working now. He keeps popping up and you keep listening to him, going with him when he wants you to. If he snapped his fingers and told you to jump through a hoop, you'd probably do it.*

"I would not," Chancy mumbled before she realized she was unconsciously lying—to herself.

TWELVE

Nate was the first of the rummage-sale searchers to announce defeat. "It's not here," he said with disgust. "The guy must have found it."

"I suppose so." Chancy covered a yawn. "Too bad."

"How about I buy you a cup of coffee on the way home?" Nate asked.

"I'd like to see you try. There aren't any all-night restaurants around here."

"No place to even get coffee?"

"Nope. Well, except maybe the gas station over in Ash Flat and I'm not even sure about that. It's a long way to drive, too. I'd ask you up to my place but…"

He gave her a long-suffering look. "I know. People would talk if we weren't chaperoned." He turned to the pastor. "How about you, Brother Logan? Want to join us?"

Noting the pained expression on Chancy's face, he immediately withdrew the invitation. "Never mind.

Chancy doesn't like to have visitors unless she's had time to spiff up her place." He raised an eyebrow. "Right?"

"Right. Especially not somebody like my pastor."

"I need to get home to my family, anyway," Logan said. "I would feel better if Nate escorted you, though."

"He has to. I rode with him." Chancy gathered up her purse and started for the door, then paused to look back at Alice and Louella. "Tell the other ladies I'll stop by after work tomorrow and help y'all straighten up this mess some more, if you need me to."

"Will do," Louella answered.

"You sure that poor little Joanna's going to be all right?" Alice asked. "You sounded pretty worried about her when you were talking to the sheriff." She smiled sweetly. "We could stop by on our way and see about her. I'm not familiar with the area you mentioned but I'm sure Louella knows how to find it."

"Thanks. I don't think that will be necessary," Chancy said. "You two must be worn out. Just go on home before the rain starts. I've been hearing thunder ever since we got here." She waved. "'Night, all."

Nate said brief goodbyes and followed her outside to the pickup. A flash of lightning illuminated the breadth of the sky. "Looks like the storm is getting closer."

"Is that your professional opinion?"

"Not officially, no. I hate to admit it but I haven't been following the weather as closely as usual."

He hesitated, watching the sky and waiting for another flash to delineate the shape of the clouds before he slid behind the wheel. He didn't want to alarm Chancy but he definitely didn't like the structure of the cloud to the southwest. The mass was black, dense and appeared have the makings of a high-precipitation super cell that could produce everything from thunder and lightning to hail to tornadoes. He'd know more once he powered up his laptop and connected to NOAA, but what he could see with the naked eye told him enough to make him decidedly uneasy.

"Well, at least it's not raining yet," she said.

Nate didn't want to be the one to tell her that a lack of rain was one of the indications of approaching trouble. It marked the main area of inflow, where warm, moist air from lower levels rose to enter the storm.

During the day he'd be able to tell more about whether there was imminent danger just by observation. At night, he had to rely on reports from the National Weather Service; reports he wasn't in a position to access at present.

"You should go home and stay inside," Nate said, trying to sound unworried for her benefit.

"I will." She sighed and rested her head on the back of the seat as he pulled out of the church parking lot. "I wish I didn't feel so responsible for what's happened. And I wish we knew what had become of that picture."

"Since we didn't find it, we have to assume the burglar has it."

"I suppose so. In that case, I guess there's nothing more we can do, is there?"

"Short of finding it ourselves, no," Nate said flatly.

"In a way, I hope the guy *did* get his hands on it because if he did, maybe he'll finally leave us alone."

"And if he didn't?"

"You know the answer to that as well as I do," Chancy told him. "If he didn't find it, he'll be back. And if he's getting half as frustrated about this whole mess as I am, he's running short of patience."

"That's not good," Nate said, shaking his head and gripping the steering wheel tightly as he drove. "That's definitely not good."

And speaking of things that were definitely not good. He caught another glimpse of the overhanging blackness as more lightning shot jagged fingers along the distant forested hills. Unless he missed his guess, their dilemma regarding the lost picture wasn't the *only* thing that was decidedly bad about that particular night.

He wasn't going to scare Chancy by warning her needlessly, but he wasn't going to go home and go to bed without first monitoring this storm's movement and assessing its potential for damage, either.

If it was going to be as bad as he thought, no one was going to get much sleep tonight.

"What do you mean it wasn't there?" Joanna asked. "It had to be. They said it was."

"Well, I didn't find it."

"Did you look everywhere?"

Sam cursed under his breath. "No. Somebody must have seen my light. A bunch of old ladies came poking around and I had to run for it. I circled back so I could watch the parking lot and I never did see anybody leaving with it."

"Then it's still there, right?"

"How should I know? You're the one who lost it."

"What're you going to do?" she asked, wilting under his menacing stare.

"Go back to the source of the whole problem and get the truth," he said. "Your boss is the key and we both know it."

"No, please."

"Oh, stop your whining. I gave you a chance to come up with the keys and you blew it." He raised his hand then laughed, clearly amused to see her sidestep.

"But, you said Chancy was at the church, too, and nobody came out with the picture. If she was there looking for it, then she must not have it, either."

"We don't know why she was there, do we?" He glowered. "Unless you tipped her off."

"I didn't. I wouldn't!"

"Then maybe she's just a busybody who likes to see what's going on. All I know is, she didn't come out of there carrying anything like your picture and neither did her boyfriend."

"He was there, too?"

"Yeah. That's why I didn't do anything at the time. No sense tipping my hand. I'll wait till she's alone and then we'll have us a nice little chat."

Joanna reached for his forearm and gripped it firmly, amazed at the sudden rush of audacity that gave her strength. "Don't you dare touch her."

Laughing, he shook her off easily. "Watch me."

In spite of the sprinkling rain that had finally begun, Chancy allowed Nate to walk her to her door, then paused to thank him. "I appreciate your concern. Really I do." She winced when a flash was followed almost immediately by booming, cracking thunder that shook the atmosphere. "Whew! That sounded close. You'd better get going before this storm gets worse."

"You sure you'll be okay? You could come home with me. I know my grandmother wouldn't mind one more houseguest."

"There's no need for that. I told you I'd changed the locks. This place is very secure now."

"Still…"

"Don't be silly. I'll lock the doors and be just fine."

"Do you have a gun?"

Chancy laughed softly. "I have a baseball bat. Will that do?" She had expected Nate to be amused. Instead, he nodded.

"Put it by your bed so it's handy in case you need it."

"You're serious?"

"Very. You don't seem to be taking these threats to heart, Chancy."

"I trust the Lord."

"Yeah, well, that's fine as long as He isn't expecting you to use the common sense He gave you."

"Now you're being facetious."

"No, I'm being practical." He reached into his pocket, took out a card and handed it to her. "This is my private cell-phone number. Call me if there's any sign of trouble."

"Instead of the sheriff?" she asked, still trying to lighten his dour mood with humor.

"I don't care if you call the whole police force as long as you call me first."

That made Chancy laugh. "I told you. The whole police force consists of two patrol cars, Sheriff Harlan, whom you've met, and his deputy."

"All the more reason why you should definitely call me. Promise?"

"Okay. I promise."

She offered her hand but instead of shaking it as

she'd assumed he would, Nate grasped and held it. His touch was warm, strong, confident.

Making no effort to pull away she stilled as she gazed into the dark, endless depths of his eyes. What was happening here? Was she imagining it or was there an unspoken connection between her and Nate that had not existed before?

It's just sweet of him to be concerned and my emotions are playing tricks on me, Chancy insisted.

"Stay safe," he whispered, closing the distance between them as he continued to hold her hand. She thought for a few seconds that he was going to bend down and kiss her but at the last instant he stepped away, instead. "Good night."

"Good night." Breathless, she watched him descend the staircase and jog back to the truck.

Her hand still tingled where he had held it and her heart seemed unable to believe there was no reason for it to continue to race. This was not good. Not good at all.

Lightning struck with a flash and a booming retort that were nearly simultaneous, telling Chancy, without a doubt, that lingering outside on the second-story landing was foolish.

She unlocked the door and quickly ducked into her apartment. Standing exposed on a high point during an electrical storm wasn't nearly as dangerous as letting Nate kiss her would have been, she decided.

She knew that conclusion was correct.

Nevertheless, she wished that he had given in and kissed her, anyway.

Nate didn't waste any time driving back to the Collins farm. He skidded to a stop in front of the house and hurried inside, taking the porch steps two at a time.

His grandparents were each seated in their respective reclining chairs in the living room and both were napping.

He touched Ted's arm to wake him before he asked, "What has the radio been saying about the weather?"

"Beats me, son." The old man yawned and peered out the window. "Looks like it's brewin' up a storm, though."

"Did the alarm go off?"

Ted frowned, looking confused. "Alarm? What alarm?"

"The SAME radio I bought you. Remember? It stands for Specific Area Message Encoder. It's to warn you of dangerous weather so you can know when to take cover."

Ted chuckled wryly. "All I got to do is look outside to tell that. Don't need no radio. Besides, it scares the fire out of your grandma when it goes off while we're sleepin'."

"That's the whole idea," Nate said.

"Yeah, I know, but you don't have to listen to her

complain afterward." He chuckled. "You're the weather expert. What's it look like to you?"

"Nasty. I'm going to power up my computer and check in with NOAA. In the meantime, you might want to stay dressed in case we have to go to the storm cellar."

Ted got stiffly to his feet and ambled over to the window. "Yup. Just might from the looks of it. Let's let Hester sleep awhile. She's plumb worn out from helpin' the ladies down at the church this afternoon."

Hesitating in the doorway, Nate said, "I didn't know she was at Serenity Chapel today. What was she doing?"

"Settin' up for the rummage sale," Ted said. "And you can tell Chancy she got that picture back for her while she was at it."

"The picture with the jewelry?" Nate tensed, his pulse beating faster. "Where is it?"

"I don't know. Around here somewhere I reckon. Why?"

"Because it may be the key to everything. I want to see it."

"Right now? I thought you were goin' to check the weather."

"I am," Nate said. "I'll go get my laptop. You find the picture and meet me in the kitchen so we don't bother Grandma while we talk about it."

* * *

Chancy hated storms. Especially noisy ones. She locked the outside door to her apartment and proceeded to turn on every light in every room, as if the added illumination would keep her emotional demons at bay.

"The Lord is my shepherd," she quoted over and over as she paced the floor and trembled. Although she loved the promises in that Psalm, she always felt a sense of foreboding when she got to the part about "walk through the valley of the shadow of death."

Death was what severe storms always reminded her of. Death and destruction. She knew entertaining unfounded fears was wrong, yet those fears persisted despite her otherwise strong faith. It was a night just like this when her parents had been killed and all the memories came flooding back as if the tragedy were about to occur all over again.

She flipped on the TV and tuned to the weather channel, hoping to see that the storm was either dissipating or passing Serenity by.

Her breath caught as the picture formed. Not only was the storm extensive, its core was moving northeast and was headed straight for the town.

Judging by the speed of the graphics, she had less than half an hour in which to secure everything and take cover!

The safest place to ride out the storm was below

in the warehouse away from windows, she reasoned. The building was brick and had withstood high winds for nearly a hundred years so it would probably do so this time, too, while the windows in her apartment were not only vulnerable they could become dangerous glass missiles if they shattered.

Another bolt of lightning hit. The electricity flickered, then failed.

Plunged into the dark except for the flashes randomly searing the sky, Chancy groped her way to the stairway leading to the shop below.

The thunder was deafening and her heart was pounding so loudly in her ears she was oblivious to any other noises.

"Please, Jesus, be with me," she prayed in a whisper.

The door at the bottom of the stairway was closed, making the passageway even more darkly ominous.

She edged her way down, one hand on the railing, the other extended to feel her way until she reached the ground floor.

The bookcase door swung open easily. Outside the wide display window she could see almost continuous bursts of light. Trees across the street on the courthouse lawn were being buffeted by severe winds and looked as if their limbs were in danger of snapping off.

"Oh, dear Lord! Watch over Nate and see him safely home," she prayed, realizing that her concern was more than that of one friend for another. She did care for him. Deeply. How ironic and unfair it would be if he were hurt by a storm when he wasn't even looking for one!

Working her way toward the storeroom, Chancy took careful, measured steps in spite of her inner desire to break into a run.

The moment she opened the connecting door between the display area and the warehouse area a strong wind hit her.

Her first thought was that the rear double doors had been blown open by the gusts.

Then, lightning flashed again and she saw a large, dark figure looming against the outside opening!

She froze. Her heart was beating so rapidly it was making her light-headed.

Duck! Hide! her mind screamed.

She couldn't move. Couldn't think. Couldn't reason. Maybe, if she stood very still, the intruder wouldn't notice her.

That hope was quickly banished. The dark figure jerked, paused for an instant, then started into the crowded room.

She saw his shadow falter and heard him curse as he stumbled over some of the boxes she'd been preparing for the rummage sale.

That was all the motivation Chancy needed to break free of her mind-numbing fear. She knew her store better than anyone and there was still at least thirty feet of crowded floor separating her from the prowler. She could escape. She *would* escape.

Already breathless, she whirled and ran.

THIRTEEN

Seated at the kitchen table with his grandfather, Nate stared at the computer screen. "They've just gone from a watch to a tornado warning for all of Fulton County," he said. "I want you and Grandma to go to the storm cellar."

"What about you?" Ted asked. "Aren't you comin', too?"

"No. I'll help you two get settled but then I'm heading back to Chancy's. I know she'll be scared and I want to tell her we have that picture back."

"You think it's really important?"

"It must be." Nate closed his laptop and stood. "Come on. Let's go."

"Domino's comin', too, even if I have to carry him."

"Of course he is. You go wake Grandma and I'll bring the dog."

"No need to wake me," Hester said from the doorway. "A body'd have to be half-dead to sleep through all this racket." She managed a smile for Nate. "I suppose there's no use tryin' to talk you out of goin' to get the girl?"

"No. If it looks too bad when I get there, we'll ride it out in town instead of coming back out here. That old brick building of hers should be pretty stable."

"It did okay in the storm of Sixty-seven," Hester said. "Broke a couple of windows but that was about all. There was a shopping mall over in Highland that lost its whole roof that year."

"Okay. Come on. You, too, Domino," Nate said, starting to herd his charges toward the back door. "Grab what you need and let's go."

"Is it raining much?" Hester asked as she reached for her coat.

Nate opened the door. "No, not much. It's still pretty warm out here, too. As soon as it cools down the worst of the danger will be past."

Ted chuckled and patted him on the back. "We know, son. We've been around storms like this all our lives. If it gets real still-like all of a sudden and the sky looks a might green, then I'll start to worry."

He led the way to the slanted metal door leading to the storm shelter and grunted with the effort as he lifted and held it. "Come on, Mama. Down you go."

"You, too," Nate said, relieving him of the weight of the door. "And call Domino."

Ted reached the bottom of the metal stairs after Hester and turned to look up at Nate and the dog. "He don't like these narrow steps much. Never did. I think you'll have to prop that door open and help him down, 'specially since he's still stove-in."

"Why am I not surprised?" Nate grumbled.

He lifted the old dog like a sack of potatoes and struggled to hand him to his grandfather without knocking all three of them into a heap. In parting, the dog arched its neck and gave him a loving slurp on the cheek.

"Ugh. Okay. I'm going to close the door now. You both okay? Got your lanterns ready?"

Hester nodded. "You take care," she called. "I'll be prayin' for you."

For the first time in longer than he could recall, Nate was truly glad to hear her say that.

He lowered the heavy door, ran back to the house for his computer and the jeweled picture, then headed for the truck. By the looks of the sky, he was going to need all the prayers he could get. And so was Chancy.

A second smaller figure found the open doors banging in the wind at the rear of the antique shop and hesitated. Sam again? Probably. He didn't have the brains to even shut the door, let alone cover his tracks in other ways. Well, no matter. The keys were the important thing. Once those were returned, Sam would be unnecessary. He didn't know it, of course, but his blunders were unacceptable to the rest of the partners. If he hadn't hidden those locker keys in the first place, he'd have gotten out of prison to find every penny of his ill-gotten gains long gone.

Struggling against the wind, the second prowler managed to secure the doors. They rattled and banged but that didn't matter. With all the racket from the storm, anyone hearing noises would assume they were normal occurrences.

Taking out a flashlight, she flipped it on and started into the warehouse.

Chancy was hunkered down behind a massive oak highboy and trying to listen for footsteps. She didn't want to be next to the display window in case it broke, nor did she want the flashes of lightning to reveal her hiding place. Normally she didn't care for the dark but in this case, the darker the better.

A narrow beam of light swept over the room, passing above her head. She held her breath. *Hide me, Jesus. Please!*

Her gaze came to rest on a nearby armoire. Was there room inside it for her to hide? She thought so. How could she get there and climb in without being seen?

The prowler kept cursing under his breath as he

worked his way through the shop. Chancy didn't like hearing such language but it was serving a good purpose because it told her approximately where he was currently searching.

Finally, he put his voice to a different use and called, "Come out and I won't hurt you. All I want is the picture with the jewelry."

She held her breath just short of an audible gasp. That *was* what he was after! Their guess had been right.

Her mood immediately plummeted. The man was already angry. He was going to be furious if and when he learned that she no longer had the collage in her possession.

The notion that he might go away and leave her alone if she told him the truth was quickly dismissed. He was obviously not the kind of person who could be reasoned with. After all, look what he'd done to poor Domino!

That thought gave her chills. Once again she eyed the armoire. Maybe, if she crawled, she could get its tall door open and slip inside without being seen. Was that the escape the Lord had arranged for her?

No, her thoughts answered clearly. *If you go in there you'll be trapped with no way out.*

But I can't stay here, she argued. *He's bound to find me eventually.*

Could she make it back to the hidden door behind

the bookcase? Should she try? Or should she work her way around after the man passed and try to sneak out the back door?

Out the door? Into that terrible storm? Which was worse, taking her chances with the elements or staying in proximity to a dangerous criminal? *What a choice!*

Chancy was trembling so badly that even her breathing was shaky. She tried to rise from a crouch and realized how weak her fear had made her.

"I trust God," she whispered, "I do." Then added, *Father, give me strength.*

The answer to her prayer for fortitude didn't come as an influx of supernatural power, it came from the sound of someone pounding on the door upstairs and shouting her name.

Nate! He didn't know about the danger from the intruder. If she didn't get to him and warn him, he could blunder into an ambush!

That was all the incentive Chancy needed. She sprang to her feet and raced for the hidden passageway.

Wind gusts were so strong Nate had to keep one hand on the railing to avoid being blown off the landing. It looked as if the electricity in that part of town was out so he couldn't be certain whether or not Chancy was still in her apartment. He had to assume she was. Anything else was unthinkable.

Intent on convincing her to accompany him back to the farm and into the storm cellar, he'd left his laptop and the jewelry collage in the truck.

Now that he was at her door, however, he was beginning to have second thoughts. This storm was building fast. Staying in the old brick building was probably wisest—if he could only get Chancy to let him in.

He was about to kick in the door when she jerked it open. Instead of inviting him inside she burst out onto the landing and straight into his arms.

"It's okay," Nate said, holding her gently but firmly. "I'm here."

She leaned back enough to stare at him. "You— you don't understand. There's somebody in the shop! It has to be the same man who hurt Domino because he said he'd come for the collage."

"What? Where is he?" Nate's embrace tightened and he tensed, bracing for a fight.

"Stuck downstairs, I hope. I don't think he saw me open the hidden door."

She clung to him, her hair whipping in the wind, her eyes filling with tears of relief. "When I heard you calling my name I was so afraid for you."

"It's all right. We'll be fine, now."

"How can you *say* that?"

"Because we're together," Nate answered as he placed a tender kiss on the top of her head.

"But, if he finds us he'll demand the collage and we don't have it."

"Yes, we do," Nate said. "Grandma got it back. It's downstairs in the truck."

"Then let's get out of here!"

He eyed the sky. Lightning was now so frequent it kept the clouds illuminated almost constantly. The wind was lessening. If he hadn't been educated about dangerous storms he might have assumed their problems were nearly over. Unfortunately, he knew otherwise.

"We can't go now. We need immediate shelter."

"But…"

Nate kept his arm around her and opened the door to her apartment. "I don't care what your neighbors think, we're going inside."

"What about the windows?"

"The safest place will be in the stairwell to your shop. It's closed on both ends and bricked up just like a safe room would be in a more modern building. We'll wait it out in there."

"What if the prowler finds us?"

Nate hurried her through the living room and into the stairway corridor. "Unless I miss my guess, our friend is going to have plenty of other things to worry about in a few more minutes."

"A tornado?"

"It's highly likely."

"Oh, my poor shop!"

He closed the upper door and led her halfway down the stairs to a central position that offered the most shelter.

"It's just a building, Chancy. It can be rebuilt. You're all I care about right now."

She lifted her face to him. He couldn't see her but he sensed her movement, felt her warm breath as she said, "Really?"

In answer, he lowered his head, found her soft lips and kissed her briefly, tenderly, before he said, "Yes. Really."

Sam was getting frantic. He crashed around the antique shop pushing over or throwing aside anything in his path that would move. She had to be here. He'd seen her once. She couldn't have gotten out past him, could she?

The storm was providing more illumination than his flashlight was so he clicked it off. That was when he noticed a thin beam coming from the direction of the warehouse.

Aha! He had her! She'd shut off her light an instant after his but it was too late. He'd spotted her. He knew exactly where she'd gone.

"You can't get away," he said hoarsely. "You might as well give me the picture."

His quarry didn't respond. He closed on her rapidly, determined to exact vengeance and retrieve his keys at the same time. "There's no use hiding. I know where you are," he threatened.

She was scared, too scared to run, he noted. Good. If she was that petrified, his job would be easy. One good slap and she'd cave just like they always did. Stupid females. None of them had a brain in their heads.

He approached.

The figure didn't budge.

He lifted his flashlight and flicked it on, aiming it at his quarry's face.

Thunderstruck, he gasped, "You!" the instant before the gun in her hand fired.

Chancy clung to Nate, unwilling to step away in spite of her misgivings about being caught alone with him in such a possibly compromising situation.

She tensed. "Listen. Did you hear that?"

"Yes. It didn't sound like the wind, did it?"

"No. It echoed. I've never heard anything quite like it before."

"I have." His hold on her remained firm. "It reminded me of a pistol shot."

"In my shop? Do you suppose the guy had a gun?"

"Probably. I'm glad he didn't use it on Domino."

"Or your grandparents," Chancy said with a shudder. "But why would he shoot?"

"Maybe he thought he saw you," Nate said.

"Thankfully, he didn't."

"Yeah."

She felt Nate release a shuddering breath and slipped her arms around his waist. "When I was praying for deliverance I never dreamed the Lord would send you," she said softly.

"Are you sure He did?"

"Absolutely."

"I did come to save you, but I didn't think it would be from an armed burglar. I knew the storm would upset you and I planned to take you to a real shelter. Too bad I got here too late."

Chancy gave him a hug and laid her cheek against his chest. "You weren't too late. I think your timing was perfect."

Downstairs, the surviving intruder gave Sam's body a kick. He didn't move. Didn't even moan.

She shone her flashlight on his face and decided he was beyond caring, so she started to rummage through his pockets. She knew he hadn't reclaimed all six keys yet but she hoped he'd brought what he did have with him. That would be a good start. And since no one else knew she was involved, she could easily lay her hands on the final few without arousing suspicion.

She'd been in a position to see the shop owner duck through a doorway and disappear, so she knew no one had seen her shoot. That was just as well. A stranger with a record, like Sam, wouldn't arouse much long-term interest in a backwater town like Serenity. Kill a local, however, and no telling how hard the sheriff would work to solve the case.

Her fingers closed on a ring of keys. She drew them out and used her flashlight to briefly check it. As she'd hoped, there were four keys that looked as if they'd fit the kind of lockers her team had planned to use to temporarily stash their loot.

Sam's arrest and subsequent jail term had meant that the secret of exactly where the money was hidden had gone to prison with him. Now, however, she had numbered keys. All she'd have to do was go to bus stations in Little Rock and Memphis and match the numbers to the proper lockers.

But first, there was the little matter of the final two keys, she reminded herself. Getting this close wasn't good enough. Even discounting Sam's share, which would now go to her and the others, there was too much money involved to just walk away and forget it.

She used the tail of her coat to wipe her fingerprints off the gun, then placed it in Sam's hand and forced his fingers closed around it. If the sheriff was as dumb as she thought he was, he'd probably never question how the man had managed to bend his arm so awkwardly and shoot himself.

* * *

Inside the stairwell, Chancy and Nate had finally relaxed enough to sit down on the steps, shoulder to shoulder, to wait.

She'd never once been afraid of him but she didn't want to tempt him too much, either. As Louella had often said, "The best way to resist temptation is to keep your hand out of the cookie jar in the first place."

"So, how long do we need to stay here?" Chancy asked.

"A little longer. It sounds like the worst has come and gone. I hear rain on the roof. You doing okay?"

"Yes, thanks. Are you sure Hester and Ted are safe?"

"I put them in the storm cellar myself," Nate replied. "Domino, too, so Grandpa won't worry about him and come out too soon."

"Good."

She hesitated, wondering if she should say what she was thinking. Finally, she decided it would be easier to discuss her feelings in the dark while Nate couldn't see her face, especially if his answers weren't the ones she expected.

"Did you mean what you said?" she asked.

"When?"

"When you told me I was all you cared about."

"Of course."

"Then I think we have a problem." Chancy breathed a noisy sigh. "Because you're all I care about, too."

"Is that so bad?"

"It might be. What are we going to do about it?"

Nate chuckled quietly. "Beats me. We're totally unsuited for each other."

"I know. Suppose we could talk ourselves out of it?"

"I doubt it. At least, I couldn't," Nate said, reaching for her hand. "I've already tried."

"Yeah, me, too." Chancy laced her fingers between his, relishing the warmth of his hand, the tenderness in his voice. "Know what the worst part is?"

"No. What?"

She giggled. "Ted and Hester are going to laugh their heads off at us."

FOURTEEN

Sheets of rain were falling at a steep angle, driven against the panes by punishing winds, when Chancy and Nate finally emerged from the safety of the stairwell.

Thankfully, the windows in her apartment were still keeping the harsh weather at bay. Lightning that had been striking so closely when they'd first taken cover was now dancing across the clouds nearer the horizon and giving the scene an eerie, patchy glow.

Chancy clapped her hands with delight when she saw the unscathed condition of her apartment. "Oh, good! I was afraid this place would be a real mess. Maybe the big display windows downstairs made it through the storm in one piece, too."

"Let's hope so."

Nate reached for his cell phone, flipped it open and held it out to her. "Speaking of what's been going on in your shop, here, call the sheriff."

"Do you think we need to?" She sobered and accepted the phone. "Never mind. You don't have to answer that. I know very well we do."

When the dispatcher answered, Chancy recognized her voice and was immensely relieved. "Oh, Sue Ann! I'm so glad it's you on duty tonight! I was afraid all the lines would be down and nobody would answer."

"We're running on backup power," the dispatcher said. "Who is this and what's your emergency?"

"Sorry. This is Chancy Boyd. I'm at my shop. There was a prowler downstairs. We thought we heard a gunshot about half an hour ago."

"Why didn't you call us immediately?"

"We were waiting out the storm in the stairwell and couldn't get a cellular signal. I guess the brick walls interfered."

"Okay. I'll send the sheriff over as soon as I can. Is the prowler still there?"

"I have no idea. I am not going back into the shop to check."

"Good girl," Sue Ann said. "If you can, it might be best to clear out and wait for Harlan over by the grocery store. I'll tell him to look for you there, okay?"

"Okay. We'll leave now."

As soon as she ended her call, Nate asked, "Leave? Why?"

"Sue Ann thinks we should get out of this building and wait for the sheriff over by the market."

Nate pressed his lips into a thin line. "I don't know about that. Right now we're relatively safe. What if whoever was downstairs realizes we're nearby and comes after us? I could probably hold my own in a fair fight but I'm not armed. Judging by what we heard, he might be."

"True."

Reliving her close call, Chancy shivered and wrapped her arms around herself. "How about we go sit in your pickup? I really want to see that collage up close. As long as we leave the motor running we should be able to make a quick getaway if we need to."

"All right. But if I find out that the storm hasn't passed the way we think it has, we're heading in the opposite direction to keep ahead of it, sheriff or no sheriff," Nate told her flatly.

"And you said *I* was stubborn."

"You are. What does that have to do with this?"

Chancy grabbed her jacket. "Nothing. You're the meteorologist so you get to call the shots in a storm. Come on. The sooner we get out of here and into that truck the better I'll like it."

"Are you still worried about busybodies thinking bad things about you because I've been in your apartment?"

"No," she said, sobering. "I'm wondering what became of a guy who was so frantic to get his picture back that he practically tore the shop apart looking for me. Suppose he's down there, just waiting for us to stick our noses out so he can shoot us?"

Nate rolled his eyes. "That was the point I was trying to make. Look, I'll go first. If it's safe, I'll start the motor, honk the horn and you can come on down."

She grabbed Nate's arm and held tight. "No way, mister. If you go, I go, too."

"Don't be ridiculous."

"What? You expect me to just stand here and let you volunteer to be the bait in a possible trap? Get real. I meant every word I said when we were stuck in the stairwell."

"So did I, which is why you're going to stay right here till I check out the access to the truck."

"Ha! That's what you think." She yanked open the door. "Let's go."

Nate quickly decided that he might as well give in. The way he saw it, the longer they stood in Chancy's apartment arguing, the greater the chance the prowler would catch up to them. As Grandpa Ted was fond of saying, "Even a blind hog finds an acorn in the forest once in a while." No matter how inept the crook might be, there was always the chance he'd accidentally stumble on their whereabouts.

Right now, Nate would have given a month's pay to have access to Ted's old twelve-gauge shotgun and a handful of double-ought-buck shells.

He turned up his jacket collar, stepped outside and began to inch his way down the wooden exterior staircase, squinting against the driving rain.

Chancy was gripping his other hand. If their nemesis was out there, Nate knew there was no way they'd spot him through this much falling water. On the other hand, there was no way the other man could get a good clear view of them, either.

Reaching the pavement, Nate broke into a run with Chancy beside him. The truck seemed to be just as he'd left it. He grabbed the passenger-side door handle, gave it a jerk and unceremoniously shoved her inside before circling and jumping behind the wheel.

The engine roared to life. "You set?"

"Yes!"

"Then hang on! I'm getting us out of here."

The wheels spun. The tires squealed. Chancy braced herself with her hands against the dashboard and her feet pressed hard to the floor.

They roared up the pothole-riddled alley, bouncing and splashing their way to the market parking lot. There was no more light there than anywhere else, much to Nate's relief.

He whipped the wheel around and slid the truck to a stop in the vacant center, its nose facing Chancy's shop.

She gasped. "What are you doing, imitating stunt drivers in the movies?"

"No. This way we'll be able to turn on the head-lights if we need to and spot anybody trying to sneak up on us."

"Unless they decide to shoot first."

"I didn't say my plan was flawless. Do you have a better idea?"

Lightning lit her face enough to show him she was giving him a wry look as she said, "No."

"Then let's concentrate on the stuff we can control. Reach under the seat and hand me my laptop, will you? That picture's under there somewhere, too."

"The way you were driving it's a wonder anything is still under the seat," she grumbled, bending over and groping along the dusty floorboard. "Yuck. Ted could plant potatoes in all the dirt under here."

"Don't even suggest it or he might try. Have you found the laptop?"

"Yes." She straightened and handed it to him, then bent again to retrieve the collage. Holding it up to let the next flash illuminate it, she frowned. "No wonder I didn't remember seeing this. It's very amateurish."

"Never mind the critique. What about it could be valuable?"

"I don't know. It doesn't look particularly remark-able. I'd have to get my jeweler's loupe and study it under better light but offhand I'd say the guy who was willing to kill to get it has to be crazy."

"That goes without saying," Nate replied. He

glanced in the rearview mirror and spotted approaching headlights. "Looks like your sheriff is here. Maybe now we'll get to the bottom of things."

Chancy huffed. "I wouldn't count on it."

Harlan had paused long enough to watch Nate check the latest real-time weather information on his laptop and pronounce the danger past, then had left them and proceeded into the antique shop. He'd instructed Chancy and Nate to stay back while he searched the building.

She was so frustrated about being left out she would have disregarded his orders in an instant if Nate had not kept insisting they should comply.

The sheriff returned in less than three minutes, walking rapidly, and went immediately to his patrol car. His wet yellow slicker glimmered red and bluish green beneath the emergency flashers on the official vehicle.

He leaned in, apparently used the radio, then returned to Chancy's side of the truck.

She rolled down the window so they could talk. "What's the report? Did you capture the guy?"

"In a manner of speaking," Harlan said. "You two care to tell me where you were while all this was going on?"

"In the stairwell. Nate thought it would be the safest place to ride out the storm. Why?"

"Neither of you left? You were together the whole time?"

Blushing, Chancy said, "Yes."

"Okay, then. I'll have to ask you to come to my office tomorrow and make a report." He peered past her at Nate. "Both of you."

"I'll need the power back on before I can do a good job of checking for damage and theft," she said. "Shall I make a list for you?"

"You can if you like," he drawled. "But mostly I'm interested in finding out who the victim was."

"Was?" She didn't like the sheriff's tone.

"Yeah, was. There's a dead body layin' smack dab in the middle of your showroom floor."

There was no way Chancy was going to agree to leave the scene without first seeing if she knew the victim. She also did not intend to resume normal life in her apartment until they knew more about the crime and the criminal.

Now that the rain had lessened, she climbed out of the truck and joined the sheriff. "I want to see him."

"You can look at the pictures we take."

"That's not good enough. I want to see everything. It's my store. I have the right to be involved."

"Not if the shooter is still around," Harlan argued. He eyed Nate and arched an eyebrow. "That is, unless you happen to already know who's responsible."

"Of course not."

"Then you'd better skedaddle and leave this to the professionals. I've called the volunteer fire department to set us up some temporary lights and the county coroner's on his way. It's gonna be a long night."

"I don't care," she said flatly. "I can wait as long as you can."

"Suit yourself. Just don't get in my way," he said, turning and heading for his patrol car.

Nate spoke up. "I should get back to the farm and check on my grandparents, Chancy. Why don't you come with me for now, let the men do their jobs, and I'll bring you back here later, whenever you say."

"I can drive myself."

"Yes, but should you?" He pointed. "Your van is parked awfully close to the building. I don't imagine the sheriff is too keen on having anybody stepping all over his clues."

She rolled her eyes. "After all this rain? Give me a break." Still, she had to concede that Nate had a good point. And his rationale also gave her the perfect excuse to remain in his company. That was the deciding factor. Staying with Nate appealed a lot more than going off on her own, especially after the close calls they'd just shared.

Chancy shrugged. "Okay. I'll ride with you to Hester and Ted's but I'm not staying. I want to be here when they wheel the guy out."

"Why? Do you think you might know him?" Nate asked.

"I don't know why I wouldn't. I know just about everybody in town."

"Harlan didn't say he recognized him."

"That's true, he didn't." Her brow knit and she glanced at the sheriff's car. "Hmm. I suppose he would have, wouldn't he? Then again, he was acting like he suspected *you.*"

Nate opened the door to his truck and held it while she got back in. "You know why, don't you?"

"Yes." She made a face. "Because you're not from around here."

The woman who now had possession of the four keys was pleased with herself. She had no doubt she'd easily be able to lay her hands on the final two and finish her job soon. That suited her just fine. The quicker she left Serenity, the happier she'd be. It was getting harder and harder to keep up the pretense of being so sweet and innocent.

She laughed at the thought. Sweet, maybe. Innocent, never. But she was good at pretending to be, wasn't she? No one ever suspected her. She had that kind of down-to-earth face, that humble, self-effacing demeanor that had always kept her out of jail, even when she'd come close to being arrested and charged with crimes in the past.

This was the first time she'd had to kill, though. Not that she hadn't wanted to do it more than once before. As far as she was concerned, most men deserved to be eliminated. Permanently. As for her other partners, they had served their purpose, too, hadn't they? Perhaps it was time to dissolve their association for good.

She smiled. That wasn't such a bad idea. First, however, she'd have to get her hands on the money and make sure she didn't need their muscle anymore. After that, there would be plenty of time to decide what else needed to be done.

Nate kept his deepest thoughts to himself as he drove toward the farm. He'd been an idiot to admit he cared for Chancy. The desperation he'd felt when he'd feared she might be in danger had pushed his emotions over the edge of reason and he'd blurted out the truth without thinking.

Well, that couldn't be helped. Neither could the fact that they were so wrong for each other. Even Chancy had admitted that, so she obviously empathized. The trick would be in deciding how to cope until he could get his grandparents moved and go back to Oklahoma for good.

He glanced in her direction. She turned her head and smiled at him. The simple, friendly gesture made Nate's stomach clench and his heart begin to race.

This was not good. Not good at all. He decided to try to distract himself by making small talk.

"So, how are you doing now?"

"Fine." She reached over and patted the back of his hand where it rested on the steering wheel. "How about you?"

"I'm great," he fibbed. "Just great. Especially since the storm front has passed."

"I know what you mean. It's interesting how you can look at that computer of yours and tell what's going to happen."

"I can come close," he said. "It's not an exact science but we're working on it. We're a lot better at predictions than we used to be, even a few years ago, especially with the new weather satellites and communications systems."

"So I gathered." She paused, then added, "I think I'd like to learn more."

His head snapped around. "Really?"

"Yes. I don't intend to become a full-fledged meteorologist like you, but there must be courses for laymen."

"There is one called Severe Weather Storm Spotter's Training. Instructors from the National Weather Service travel around the country and teach it in local areas."

"That sounds perfect."

"You're serious? You're not just saying that?"

"Why would I?"

"To try to please me, I guess."

Chancy laughed. "I may be a simple country girl but I'm not naive enough to think I need to change my basic beliefs in order to impress you. I am what I am. What you see is what you get."

"Same here. And since you mentioned it, you should know that I'm never going to stop chasing storms."

"I know that. I'd never ask you to."

"You wouldn't? I thought…"

"I thought so, too, until tonight. When I saw what you could do, how you could help folks like Ted and Hester stay safe, I guess I started to see your job a little differently." Her smile widened to a grin. "Of course, that doesn't mean I won't still worry about you, even after you go back to Oklahoma."

"You could think about coming with me," he suggested, holding his breath for her answer.

Chancy shook her head slowly, pensively. "No. Sorry. Serenity is my home. It always has been. I could never leave here."

"I guess I knew that. I was just hoping…"

"You fly your own plane. There's no reason why you couldn't visit often. At least you'd always know where to find me."

"Yeah. But that's a lousy way to build a marriage."

He heard her gasp, saw her fingertips press to her lips. "A—a, what?"

"Don't panic. I wasn't proposing. We hardly

know each other yet. I just meant I've seen other couples try to get along long-distance and it hasn't worked for them."

Chancy's smile returned. "Whew! You scared me for a second there."

"That doesn't mean we can't be friends, does it?"

"Of course not."

Nodding, Nate went back to concentrating on the road ahead. He knew better than to think he and Chancy could ever be mere friends. The more they were together, the more his feelings for her would deepen. Chances were, her feelings for him would, too. The kindest thing he could do for either of them was to make himself scarce.

Logically, he knew that. Emotionally, it tore him up to even consider doing it.

FIFTEEN

Chancy had apparently dozed off on Hester's sofa because when she awoke to the wonderful aromas of a country breakfast, she was lying there, covered with a hand-crocheted afghan.

It took her a few moments of disorientation to realize just where she was and to recall who and what had brought her to the farm.

"Morning, sleepyhead," Hester said amiably. "You hungry?"

"Um." She stretched and yawned. "I wasn't until I smelled food. What are you fixing?"

"Bacon, eggs and homemade biscuits," the older woman answered. "Coffee, too, of course." She leaned down and peered out the front window. "Good thing I made plenty. Looks like Harlan's here, too."

Chancy sat bolt upright and rubbed her eyes. "What time is it?"

"Nearly eight. The rest of us have been up for hours. You were sleepin' so sound we decided to let you be."

"Oh, no. I wanted to watch when they brought the victim out of my shop so I could see if I knew him."

"No harm done," Hester insisted. "I'm pretty sure he's not goin' anywhere. Besides, after the terrible time you had last night you needed your rest."

"That's probably true." Chancy got to her feet, straightened her clothing and proceeded to neatly fold the afghan. "Where's everybody else?"

"The fellas went over to the airport to check on Nate's plane and see how it fared during the storm."

"Oh, dear. I'd forgotten all about that. I hope it's okay."

"Me, too." Wiping her hands on her apron, she went to answer the polite knock on the front door. "Morning, Sheriff. You're just in time for breakfast."

He doffed his hat. "I can't stay, Miss Hester. Is Chancy Boyd here?"

"That, she is. Go right on in."

As soon as they'd exchanged greetings, Chancy asked, "Are you done with my store?"

"Yup. All finished. I have pictures of the victim out in the car. Would you mind taking a quick look?"

"No. Not at all. Hold on a sec." Dashing back into the living room, she returned with the small collage. "You'll probably want this since the prowler said he was after it, but I can't for the life of me figure out why."

He accepted it gingerly. "Is it valuable?"

"Well, not the jewelry, if that's what you're asking. I looked it over last night, after Nate and I got back here, and I don't think there's ten dollars' worth there, even if it wasn't sitting in gobs of hot glue."

"Why didn't you give this to me last night?" His bushy eyebrows raised.

"Truth to tell, I didn't even think of it. I don't often have dead bodies in my store. Guess I had other things on my mind." She smiled at him. "Anyway, you have it now so no harm done, right?"

"I guess not. I will need you to sign a statement that it passed from your possession into evidence."

"Gladly. I'm thrilled to be rid of it."

She raked her fingers through her tangled hair and realized how disheveled she must look after her ordeal. Unfortunately, she hadn't thought to even grab her purse when she and Nate had fled the night before.

"Are you headed back to town right now?" she asked the sheriff.

"Soon as you look at the coroner's pictures. Why?"

"I thought maybe I could hitch a ride with you."

"Sure."

Chancy turned to Hester. "I appreciate everything you all have done for me but I really need to get home. Do you mind terribly if I don't stay to eat breakfast?"

"Bless your heart. Of course not. I'll fix you both

a hot biscuit sandwich to take along. Don't you go away. I'll just be a minute."

Chancy was glad she'd chosen to ride back to town with Harlan. Although she and Nate had had no further opportunity to discuss the particulars of their personal conversation the night before, she was embarrassed to have made such a fool of herself.

Her imagination had run away with her the moment he'd mentioned marriage and her reaction had given away far too much. He'd been right when he'd said they hardly knew each other. Could she possibly have fallen in love with him so quickly?

Yes, she answered honestly. She didn't know how or why such an illogical bond had formed, she only knew that it had. She loved Nate Collins. It was that simple. And that confusing. As a result, the kindest, most loving thing she could do was to try to subdue her true feelings, especially when he was around.

Harlan hadn't asked her nearly as many questions as she'd expected him to during the short ride back to Serenity, thanks in part to having his mouth full of Hester's delicious portable breakfast.

He pulled to a stop at the curb in front of the brick building housing Chancy's Second Chances and left the motor idling. "Want me to go in with you?"

"No. I'm fine. It just feels a little funny, that's all. You're sure there's nothing I can hurt if I clean the place up?"

"Nope. It's all yours. We're finished. If you think of anything else that might help us figure out what that man was up to before he shot himself, give me a call."

"Right. Will do." She smiled at him as she climbed out. "And thanks for telling me you don't suspect Nate anymore."

He touched the brim of his Smokey Bear hat and nodded. "Just doing my job, Miss Chancy. You and that Collins fella, you gonna keep seein' each other?"

"I don't know. I don't think so."

"Just as well," Harlan said. "Well, if you're okay I'll be on my way."

"I'm good. Take care."

"You, too."

She paused to watch him cruise slowly down the quiet street and make a tight turn at the corner of the square.

The parklike lawn around the courthouse was littered with broken branches and shredded green leaves but all in all the downtown area had fared pretty well, considering.

Harlan had informed her that a small twister had touched down in the woods off Highway 9, sparing the town and the electric co-op had already restored power. That meant life could get back to normal. Most life, anyway.

Sighing, she turned and entered the antique shop that had been both her business and her home. To her dismay and sadness, the pleasure she usually experienced upon arriving there was missing. So was her sense of peace.

She continued toward the office, careful to skirt the area where Harlan had said the man's body had been found. The investigators had obviously taken the rug he'd landed on, too. As far as she was concerned, they could keep it. Even if the stains could be washed out, she'd never be able to bring herself to sell it to anyone, not knowing what she did about its recent history.

And speaking of history, she mused, why was it that her every act, every thought, brought images and remembrances of Nate? She could vividly picture him in the shop, on the stairs, everywhere. It was as if, no matter how far she ran or how much distance she put between them, he was always right there with her.

Would it always be so? she wondered. Probably. Just as she would probably always visualize the photos of that horrible sight in the middle of her showroom floor.

She shivered and folded her arms close to stifle the chill. They were no closer to figuring out exactly why a stranger had broken into her store than they had been before he'd shot himself. Nor did they know why the collage was so important to him.

Harlan had speculated that perhaps the jewelry might have come from a robbery, but when Chancy had examined it at Hester's house, she'd concluded that it was cheaply made and had no value, not even as a collectible.

Deciding that she'd feel better about everything if she gave both herself and the shop a thorough scrubbing, she headed toward her apartment to take a much-needed shower and freshen up.

Her head hurt. Her heart was overburdened. And her poor brain was as befuddled as it had ever been.

"Trust in the Lord with all your heart and lean not onto your own understanding," she quoted, making a face for her own benefit.

This whole confusing mess was driving her crazy. And it didn't look as if things were going to get better anytime soon.

Well, at least the bad guy was out of the picture, she reasoned. For that she was extremely thankful. Given enough time, she was certain she'd be able to subdue her memories of him lying in a pool of blood in the middle of her floor.

What she didn't want to forget was the way Nate had arrived to save her, to look after her, even though she knew she'd probably have muddled through just fine on her own.

It wasn't that she needed attention, it was that she wanted someone to care. More than that, she wanted him to be the one.

Such dreams weren't sensible. They weren't even plausible. Yet there they were, as unmistakably clear as the blue sky and as warm as the summer sun.

"Father, I have a problem," she prayed as she started up the stairs to her apartment. "Help?"

Chancy was mopping the showroom floor when the tinkling of the bell over the door made her look up. Louella, Trudy Lynn, Carol Sue, Alice and Melody came trooping in. Before they were through the door, they were joined by Joanna.

Chancy leaned on the mop handle and grinned. "Hi, everybody. Did y'all come to check out the scene of the crime? Maybe I should charge admission. My phone's been ringing so much this morning I quit answering it. Everybody wants all the gory details." She rolled her eyes. "I've had calls from people I haven't talked to in years."

"How funny," Louella said with a lopsided grin. "I'm glad you still have your sense of humor. Actually, we came to help you clean the place up. At least some of us planned to." Her gaze came to rest on Joanna. "You, too?"

The girl looked decidedly uncomfortable. "I'll be glad to help if I'm needed."

"The more the merrier," Chancy said brightly. "I only have one mop but there's a vacuum in the closet back there and plenty of dust rags. Make yourselves at home."

"I don't dust much at my house," Louella quipped, "but I think I can remember how. Come on, girls. There's work to be done."

"Aren't you going to tell us what happened first?" Melody asked.

Trudy Lynn and Carol Sue hung back to add their own queries. "Yes! Do tell. We're dying to hear the whole story."

"Now, girls," Alice said with a look of mature forbearance. "There's plenty of time for that. Right now we need to get Chancy's store back in order. It looks like the police tracked in buckets of mud."

"They sure did. Y'all won't believe what happened," Chancy said, glad for the company and eager to unwind by talking about her harrowing experiences with such close friends. "I'd just come down from upstairs, looking for a safe place to ride out the storm last night, when I noticed that the back door wasn't closed like it was supposed to be."

"Did it blow open?" Louella asked.

"That was what I thought at first. Then I saw a man standing there."

"You actually *saw* him?"

"Yes. His shadow, anyway. He was yelling about

a picture he wanted me to give him, only I didn't have it. All I could do was hide and hope he didn't find me."

"Oh, you poor thing! What then?"

"I heard a voice. Nate's voice," Chancy said, blushing and looking toward the stairway as if seeing a replay of the prior night's events. "I didn't want him to blunder into the store and get hurt so I made a run for it."

Melody and Joanna both gasped. Alice was shaking her head. "You're one lucky girl. He could have shot you."

"I didn't know he had a gun at the time," Chancy said. "We only found out about that later. The sheriff thinks he must have tripped in the dark and accidentally shot himself."

Her gaze came to rest on the section of the floor she'd been mopping. "Nate and I heard the shot but we couldn't get a signal to use his cell phone to call the sheriff until we got out of the stairwell."

Louella arched her trim brows. "What, pray tell, were you two doing in there?"

"Using it as a makeshift storm cellar," Chancy explained. "I'd never thought about it before but it makes perfect sense. There are no windows and the walls are brick. Unless the whole building came down around me, that's the safest place I could be."

"Yes, unless you were stuck in there with a handsome hunk like Nate Collins," Louella teased. "I'll go get that dust rag you mentioned but when I get back I want to hear every last detail."

"There's nothing more to tell," Chancy insisted.

Except for Joanna, everyone else giggled in response. Chancy studied the girl's pale face, noting the dark circles under her eyes. Clearly, she'd been suffering. Somehow, the members of Louella's Extraordinary Ladies' Sunday School Class were going to have to break through the poor girl's defenses and find out what was wrong so they could help her. Somebody sure had to.

The shop was in order by midmorning. Chancy hung an Out to Lunch sign on the door and invited the makeshift cleaning crew to her apartment for refreshments.

Only Joanna hesitated. "I—I really can't stay."

"Nonsense," Chancy said. "You worked as hard as everybody else. Come upstairs and have a glass of iced tea with us."

"No, I... Could I have a word with you? Privately?"

"Sure." Chancy waved the others off. "Go on up. I'll be there in a sec."

She took the girl aside and spoke to her quietly. "What is it? Can I help you?"

"No, but I think I can help you," Joanna whispered. "It's about the collage."

"The one with the jewelry?"

"Yes. Where is it? Do you know?"

Chancy nodded slowly. Her brow furrowed. "Yes. Why?"

"You need to get rid of it or you'll never be safe. Give it to me and I'll take care of it."

"I don't think that's such a good idea. If it's dangerous for me to have it, it will be just as dangerous for you."

"No it won't. I'll take it back to where it belongs and you'll never hear from me again. I promise."

"Suppose you tell me what this is all about?"

The young woman shook her head emphatically. "I can't."

"Why not? What are you afraid of?" Chancy didn't like the wary look on Joanna's face or the way her eyes darted around the shop as if she were expecting imminent attack.

"And don't tell me you're not afraid because I can see you're scared silly."

"That doesn't matter. Nothing does, anymore. Just give me my picture and I'll go."

"*Your* picture? Are you the artist?"

Joanna nodded. "Yes. You have to give it to me. My life depends on it!"

"I wish I could help you but I don't have it," Chancy said. "The sheriff does. I'm not sure how long he's going to want to keep it. Why don't we go see him and you can tell him why you need it so

badly? I'm sure he'll be lenient if you explain everything. And I'll stand by you."

"No. You don't understand. I can't."

It occurred to Chancy that the frantic young woman
could have had a hand in the demise of the prowler. If
so, she might have acted in Chancy's defense. "Look.
If you were here last night during the storm…"

Joanna's eyes widened. She held her hands in
front of her, palms out, and began to back away.
"Forget it. I'm sorry I said anything. I have to go."

Thunderstruck, Chancy watched her bolt for the
door, jerk it open and race out.

When she turned to follow the others up to her
apartment, she saw that they had crowded into a knot
at the foot of the stairs, taking it all in as if watching
a riveting episode of their favorite soap opera. She
couldn't blame them. That was exactly what her life
was beginning to remind *her* of.

Louella shook her head. "Poor thing."

Agreeing, the others echoed the sentiment.

"Surely, there's some way we can help her," Alice
said kindly as they all began to climb the stairs together.

Chancy was bringing up the rear. "That's exactly
what I was thinking."

Nate was more than a little disconcerted to learn
that Chancy had left his grandparents' house with
Harlan instead of waiting for him to take her back to

town. He'd questioned his grandmother about it, trying to figure out whether or not Chancy had been in trouble with the law, but Hester hadn't been able to shed much light on the situation.

He'd tried repeatedly to phone the antique shop with no success and was growing more frustrated by the minute. Where could Chancy be? Why wasn't she answering her phone? Could she actually have been arrested and the sheriff had fooled his grandmother to spare her the anxiety?

That hypothesis made no sense to Nate.

He gritted his teeth. Surely, if Chancy was with the sheriff she was safe, yet he couldn't help wondering and worrying. It didn't matter how many times he assured himself that the crisis must be over, he couldn't quite believe it. That disbelief left him decidedly uneasy and short-tempered, especially with himself.

He'd been over and over all the details in his mind and was no closer to solving the riddle than he had been before. If the jewelry in the picture wasn't valuable, as Chancy had determined, then why had the dead man been so intent on reclaiming it? And why did his untimely demise seem a bit too convenient?

Nate knew he should report back to work in Oklahoma and let all the intrigue and confusion in Serenity wait until he had time to deal with it properly. He also knew that leaving was out of the question. Even if he'd been under the threat of losing his job, he couldn't have abandoned Chancy without first being certain she was safe—and was going to remain that way.

Brooding, he paced and waited for her to phone and tell him what was going on. Finally, he grew so frustrated he left the house to seek solitude in the barn. That was where he'd often gone as a teen when he'd been confused or had felt disconnected from the rest of the world. Its naturally peaceful atmosphere reminded him of the fleeting calm he'd occasionally experienced while in church and it was the place where he'd poured out his heart to God before he'd even known for sure whether or not he believed.

The weathered wooden door was propped open and hung unevenly on rusted hinges. Sunlight filtered through a rectangular gap in the sheet-metal roof and warmed the interior while dust motes danced in the beams.

Alone as he had hoped, Nate stepped into the light and closed his eyes. There was no spiritually uplifting prayer on his lips, nor did he have a clue what he should ask.

Only one thing was clear. His heart was filled with confused thoughts of Chancy and his soul craved the kind of respite only God could provide.

"Lord, I'm stuck here," he murmured. "I don't

know what to do or where to go. I could sure use a little advice."

He took a deep breath and released it as a sigh. Logical thought usually governed his life but it was useless in this situation. All he really wanted to do was to go to Chancy. To see for himself that she was okay. To ask her why she'd left the farm so abruptly.

Following her to town would mean swallowing his pride and taking the chance she'd changed her mind about him, yet he knew he had to do it. If she rejected him, so be it. There was always the chance that she'd been as serious about her feelings for him as he'd been when he'd told her how much she meant to him.

Deciding on his next course of action, Nate left the barn, climbed into the truck and headed for town.

He wasn't going to try to push Chancy into any kind of binding promise; he simply needed to be sure she was okay and find out where he stood with her at that moment.

If, as he hoped, she thought there might be a chance for them to find happiness together, fine.

If not, he needed to know that, too.

SIXTEEN

After Chancy had bid her friends goodbye she'd been unable to stop thinking about what Joanna had said. The collage was the key to the puzzle, all right. But why?

Pacing, she went over and over everything the frightened girl had told her and all she got for her efforts was a pounding headache.

The sheriff's office was less than a block away and the weather was balmy so she decided to lock up early and stroll over to see if Harlan's investigation was making any progress.

She found him in his office, seated behind a desk piled with so much paper it looked as if his file cabinets had exploded. "Afternoon, Sheriff."

"Afternoon, Chancy. Any more trouble?"

"Not exactly." Crossing to the only usable chair, she cleared it of a stack of junk mail and sat down. "I did have an interesting chat with Joanna Jones, though."

"The girl you asked me to check on the other night?" He leaned back and stretched wearily.

"The same. She said that collage the guy was after was hers. And she was pretty insistent that she had to have it back, or else."

That perked him up. "Or else, what?"

"She didn't say. But she sure was acting nervous. When I told her you had it, she panicked and left the shop."

"That's all?"

"Pretty much. I was wondering, do you suppose we should give it to her and see what she does with it?"

Thoughtful, he drew his fingers over his chin. "Can't do that. We'd lose the chain of custody and the evidence would be worthless in court. Even if I could give it to her, I wouldn't. What if she got away from us?" His brow knit. "Do you think she might have killed your prowler?"

"I thought you said he accidentally shot himself."

"That's what we thought, until we got to lookin' a tad closer. There were no powder burns on him."

"Uh-oh." Chancy's eyes widened, her heart beating faster. "It wasn't an accident?"

"Doesn't look like it. Which brings me back to the girl," Harlan said, starting to rise. "I think I'd better go have a talk with her."

"Before you do, can I see the collage again?"

"Sure. Got it right here." He sat back down, unlocked his desk drawer, withdrew the collage and passed it to her. "Just don't take it out of the plastic."

"Why not? I'm the one who handed it to you in the first place." She gave him a lopsided smile. "You have dusted it for prints, haven't you?"

"Yes. And there were so many smudged all over it we couldn't use any of them."

Chancy chuckled. "No wonder. Probably half the women in Serenity Chapel and everybody at the auction touched it. So did Hester." She was peering at the jewelry. "It's really hard to see well this way. Are you sure I can't take it out of the bag?"

He shrugged. "Oh, all right. Just be careful with it."

"I will."

Harlan quietly hovered and watched Chancy examining the paste-and-jewelry conglomeration.

"I still can't see the value," she finally said. "This thing has to be the key, but... Wait a minute." She started to pry at a brass-colored object nestled against the fabric background. "Hold everything. I think maybe..."

"What?" The sheriff leaned down to get a closer look. "What have you got?"

"Keys," Chancy said excitedly. "I kept telling myself this picture had to be the key but I never noticed before that there were *real* keys in with the junk jewelry." She held up the ones she'd freed from the glue then placed them in his outstretched hand.

"There. What do you think? Could those be what everybody's been after?"

"It's a possibility. Finding where they fit or why they're important will be like looking for a needle in a haystack, though."

"Not if we give them back to Joanna."

"I can't do that, Chancy. I already told you. That whole picture thingie is evidence in a murder."

She started to grin. "What if we substitute different keys, ones that look enough like those to fool people? I have a ton of old brass keys back at the shop. I'm sure I can find some that will fit right into these empty places. All we'll have to do is make them stick and nobody will be able to tell we've made the switch."

"Tamper with evidence?" He was scowling. "You've already messed with it too much. Besides, what good will it do to make a substitution?"

"Well, for starters, you'll have the real keys loose so you can start tracing them. And whoever was after this picture will think they're still undiscovered so you'll have plenty of time to round up suspects without anybody getting wise and running off."

"No way. I can't let you get involved."

"Ha! I'm already involved up to my eyebrows and you know it. The sooner we get to the bottom of this, the safer I'll be."

He stood firm and shook his head. "No."

"At least let me provide substitute keys for you. I can do that, can't I?"

"Okay. I'll go that far. But no shenanigans." He dropped the keys Chancy had discovered into the now-empty evidence bag and returned it to the locked drawer.

"Cross my heart," she promised, cradling the collage as she got to her feet and headed for the door.

"Hey! Where do you think you're going with that?"

"To my shop. It'll only take me a few minutes to stick replacements in the empty spaces."

The sheriff was already striding across the room. "No way, missy. If that thing leaves this office I go with it. I have to maintain the legal chain of custody, remember?"

"Fine. Then come with me."

He opened the office door and held it for her. "Okay, but no glue. We don't add anything to that picture except substitute keys, you hear? You can just lay them on there to see what fits and we'll take them right off again, keep them separate but handy, just in case I need to show the picture to one of my suspects and see what he or she does."

"Understood," Chancy said.

The observer smiled. Appealing to Chancy's sense of fairness had done the trick, hadn't it? She'd gone and gotten the collage from the sheriff and it was therefore no longer under lock and key. The most amazing fact was that the lawman had let her take it out of his office, even if he was accompanying it.

Well, there was no time to waste. The sooner she got her hands on it and split, the sooner this whole episode could be put behind her.

She decided to drive around the block and leave her car by the market where it would be less likely to be noticed. There was no sense getting careless when success was within reach. As long as no one knew why the collage was valuable, she wouldn't have to resort to violence again. That was just as well. The less fuss she made, the easier her ultimate escape would be.

The first order of business was to separate Chancy Boyd from the sheriff.

Nate had cruised by the front of the antique store and had seen the Closed sign in the window, so he proceeded through the alley, parked by the warehouse and took the stairs to Chancy's apartment two at a time.

She didn't answer his knock. He tried the door and found it unlocked, much to his chagrin. Hadn't her brush with a dangerous prowler taught her anything?

He eased it open and called, "Chancy? You here?"

No one answered. If he hadn't been so worried about her welfare he would have stayed outside, but something told him he should investigate. "Chancy?"

The door at the top of the hidden staircase was closed. He quietly opened it and listened. Voices were coming from the shop below. Women's voices. One was clearly Chancy's. The other, he didn't recognize.

Normally, Nate would have announced his presence and joined them. This time, however, he decided against it.

Starting down the stairs, he took care to proceed quietly and ease his weight from step to step rather than let a squeaking board draw undue attention to his presence.

He reached the bottom in time to hear the unknown woman say, "I'm sorry to have to do this, dear, but since you've figured it out I have no choice."

Chancy could hardly breathe. How could such a sweet, innocent-looking person be so evil?

"Look. Just take the picture and the keys. I won't say a word, I promise." She held out her hand and displayed the two brass keys she'd chosen as replacements for the real ones moments before her nemesis had barged in, hit poor Harlan over the head and then accosted her at gunpoint.

"You know I can't do that."

"Why not? I don't know what they open and neither does the sheriff."

"Then what was he doing here?"

"He just came along to be sure I was okay."

She snorted derisively. "You're a terrible liar, you know. That figures. You church people are all alike."

"But, you and I met there. You seemed so nice, so loving. Surely, you must have some sense of right and wrong."

"All I know is that the guy with the biggest stick wins," she said wryly. "Especially if he's halfway bright instead of an idiot like Sam was."

"Sam?"

The woman's gaze flitted momentarily to the place on the showroom floor where the body had lain. "You met Sam the other night. Remember?"

Chancy shivered. "You and he were working together?"

"In a manner of speaking. Sam had the keys to my future until he left them with his stupid wife and she lost them."

"Wife? Who?"

"Joanna."

"They were married?"

"Yes. It would have been much easier if she'd managed to retrieve them all before everything got so complicated."

The pistol remained pointed at Chancy. Only the wooden sales counter stood between her and the gun.

Chancy knew that if she merely ducked behind the

counter there would be no way she could escape without being wounded. Or worse.

The two keys were still displayed on her open palm. Below, in a drawer that stood slightly open, lay dozens of similar keys. She eased one step back.

"Freeze. Don't move."

"I—I feel faint."

"Well, get over it," the woman said, reaching toward her. "Give me those keys. Now."

Chancy used her free hand to yank the drawer open and at the same time dropped the loose keys into the jumble as she dove for cover.

As she'd hoped, her adversary's attention was momentarily diverted.

The woman lunged for the drawer and came up with a useless handful of similar keys. Cursing and screeching, she threw them down and started after Chancy.

Nate burst from behind the bookcase and into the fray. He didn't know who the older woman was but he'd heard enough to figure out that she was anything but the sweet middle-aged lady she pretended to be. Not only was she cursing like a pro, she was brandishing a snub-nosed, nickel-plated revolver as if she fully intended to use it.

It didn't take a genius to deduce that she needed to be stopped. Immediately. His biggest problem was his instinctive reluctance to harm a woman.

Then, he saw her extend her arm and draw a bead on Chancy and all his inhibitions disappeared.

He shouted. "Hey!"

She whirled.

The gun fired at him instead.

Chancy screamed, "No!" as Nate crumpled.

He wasn't certain exactly what happened after that because his vision was blurred by pain. It looked as if Chancy had grabbed an armless chair and was swinging it like a baseball bat!

He didn't know what she intended to accomplish but her efforts were certainly making a shambles of their surroundings. And, to her credit, of the attacker, as well.

There was a cracking sound that could have come from the wooden chair or from its contact with the back of the gun-wielding woman's skull. Either way, she collapsed in a heap and the pistol went flying.

Nate closed his eyes for an instant as another spasm of pain ran up his arm and into his shoulder.

Hearing a man's shout, he looked up in time to see the sheriff rise from the floor where he'd been lying, apparently unconscious, and draw his gun.

Chancy dropped the chair and fell to her knees beside Nate while Harlan holstered his weapon and reached to help the gray-haired woman who was struggling to get to her feet a few yards away.

"No! Grab her!" Chancy shouted frantically. "She's the murderer."

Harlan froze, his hand on the woman's arm. "This lady? You sure?"

"Yes," Chancy said, choking back sobs. "Call an ambulance. She shot Nate."

Chancy had pressed a hand towel over Nate's bleeding bicep and had tried to make him comfortable while they waited for medical help. She caressed his cheek. Tears trickled down her face and she brushed them away.

"That was a really stupid thing to do," she said, managing a smile when the corners of his mouth lifted, too. "Brave, but stupid."

"That's me," he replied. "Wouldn't you know it, I risk my life all the time on the job and then I get hurt when I'm off duty."

"Harlan says it's not serious."

Nate chuckled and grimaced. "Oh, yeah? Well, tell him it hurts plenty, just the same." Holding the towel in place against the wound, he tried to peer past her to see what was going on. "Who was that crazy woman?"

"Alice Franks, or so she told us. I suppose that was a lie, too. Everything else about her was."

"Was she in cahoots with the guy who was killed?"

"That's what she said." Chancy had to step back

to make room for the paramedics to tend to Nate but she stayed as close as possible and continued to explain. "That jewelry collage was the key, just like we thought, only not in the way we figured."

"I don't get it."

"I'll tell you everything later, after they patch you up at the hospital," she said tenderly. "You just hang in there, okay?"

He gave her the most endearing smile she had ever seen as he said, "Honey, as long as you're all right I'm the happiest guy in Arkansas."

"I'd like it better if you were in one piece," she quipped, hoping the sincerity of her comment came through.

"I'll heal," Nate replied. "And when I do, you and I are going to have a serious talk about the future. Our future."

"Is that a threat or a promise?"

Laughing, Nate winced as he answered, "Both."

Nate hadn't had to spend the night in the hospital and neither had Harlan, although the lawman had sustained a slight concussion.

Chancy had driven Nate home to the Collins farm where his grandparents had greeted him with love and had bombarded him with questions.

"I don't know," he said in answer to Hester's query about the criminals' backgrounds. "Ask Chancy. She talked to the sheriff while I was getting this arm bandaged." He reached for her and she gladly took his free hand.

"Harlan thinks it was a robbery ring," she explained. "Sam, the guy who was killed in my shop, was one of the men involved. He hid some stolen money that belonged to him and his partners, just like he was supposed to, but before he could pass out the keys to any of the others, he was arrested."

"And his girlfriend hid the keys?" Hester guessed.

"Actually, Joanna was his wife. The poor thing was innocent of any real wrongdoing. All she did was use some interesting things to make collages. We thought the jewelry was what was valuable but it turned out that she'd glued some of her husband's keys into her artworks, too. That little picture from the Hawkinses' sale had two of them stuck to it."

"Mercy! No wonder everybody was after it."

"I'm just sorry you had to be involved," Chancy said, feeling Nate's fingers give hers a squeeze. "But now that Alice is in custody and talking her head off to make a deal, the sheriff assures me the rest of the gang won't escape, either. If I'd had any idea what was going on, I'd never have given you that picture."

"No harm done," Hester replied. "We all know the Lord works in mysterious ways. Besides, it served its purpose. It brought you two kids together."

"Kids?" Chancy giggled. "We're a little older than that, Miss Hester."

The elderly woman caught her grandson's attention and winked at him. "Old enough to make a few serious decisions, I reckon. What about it, Nate, you gonna propose to this gal or drag your feet for ages like your grandpa did with me?"

Ted coughed. "I did not drag my feet. Things moved along plenty fast once we started courtin'."

"Fast? I was nearly done sewin' my wedding dress before you even figured out what was goin' on!"

Their spirited exchange made both Chancy and Nate laugh. Their glances met, softened, spoke an understanding without words.

"We'll work it out," Nate said. "I don't know the details yet but we'll definitely work it out. Maybe I can fly back and forth to Oklahoma, the way Chancy suggested, and the rest of you can stay right here."

Grinning, Chancy nodded. "We'd like that very much. Very, very much."

"You mean you're goin' to stop trying to make your grandma and me move?" Ted asked, sounding relieved. "We can keep livin' here, like always?"

"If that's what you want to do, it's fine with me," Nate said. "I was just trying to help you the way you'd helped me."

"When we're done here we'll let you know, okay?"

Ted began to grin as he caught his wife's eye. "Say, Mama, how about we give these two kids a section of the farm so's they can build a house on it? I was thinkin' of that grove of oaks over on the east side by the creek. It's real pretty there. What do you think?"

Hester bent closer to kiss his cheek. "You're an old softy and I love you for it. That's a wonderful idea."

"We couldn't accept a gift like that," Chancy said.

"Nonsense. It'll be our wedding present to you both," Ted insisted. "Besides, this'll all be yours when we're gone, anyway."

"Well, that settles it," Nate said, gazing at Chancy and smiling. "If we're going to be landowners, we'll have to stay. And if we're going to be building a house, I guess you'll have to marry me, whether you like it or not, or the gossips in town will have a field day."

She returned his smile and nodded, her vision misting with happy tears. "I guess I will. You sure you won't mind commuting?"

"Not when I have such a great family to come home to," he said. "Was that a yes?"

"Oh, yeah," she said, breaking into a cheek-splitting grin. "That was a definite yes."

EPILOGUE

Rather than use a commercial florist to decorate for her wedding, Chancy had let the Extraordinary Ladies' Sunday School Class adorn the sanctuary of Serenity Chapel with every spare flower they could muster.

Given their eclectic tastes, that meant some unusual displays, including mop-headed hydrangeas from the Collins farm, potted geraniums from Trudy Lynn's porch and pale pink-and-white orchids waving on spindly stems, fresh from Carol Sue's greenhouse.

Chancy, in keeping with her love of antiques, had chosen an off-white satin gown edged with handmade lace that had been part of an estate she'd recently purchased.

Her bouquet was composed of more homegrown flowers, some still bearing a smattering of unlucky insects.

She blew on the bouquet, shook it and laughed as

she waited in the anteroom with Becky Malloy and Louella Higgins, her attendants.

Louella took the bouquet from Chancy and, holding it at arms' length, headed for the door. "I'll go give this a good shake outside. Be right back," she said with a chuckle.

Becky patted Chancy's hand. "You doing okay?"

"Wonderful. After ducking tornadoes and crooks and Nate being shot, getting married should be easy," she answered. "I can hardly wait."

"Is he really going to keep commuting all that way?"

"For the present," Chancy said. "I'd never ask him to give up work that he feels is so important. Maybe later, when we're older, he'll decided to transfer to an office that's closer to home."

Becky sighed. "I know the Lord gives us every good and perfect gift but His plans continue to amaze me. I never would have imagined that you and Nate would turn out to be so right for each other." She smiled wistfully. "But you are. I've never seen a couple more in love." Her smile grew. "Except maybe for me and my Logan."

"I didn't think this kind of happiness was possible, considering the way my parents acted when I was growing up," Chancy admitted, "and neither did Nate."

"His childhood was turbulent, too?"

"Yes, but now that we've spent a lot more time with Hester and Ted, I can imagine exactly how Nate and I will behave when we've been together as long as they have."

"Speaking of time," Becky said, motioning Louella to hurry back with the bouquet. "It's time to go. I hear the wedding march music."

Chancy accepted her flowers, stood tall and followed her attendants into the sanctuary.

The pews were crowded with well-wishers but she had eyes for only one person.

Once she spotted her handsome future husband, waiting for her at the foot of the aisle, she could have been stepping into the eye of an F-5 tornado and she wouldn't have noticed.

He looked at her. He smiled.

Her heart's desire carried her forward as if she were floating on air. Nate was waiting for her. He loved her. That was all she needed to know.

Dear Reader,

There are many things in life that don't turn out the way we've planned or the way we wish they would. No one but God has the divine insight necessary to look ahead and see what the future holds for each of us, which is why I've decided to place my life in His hands. I still argue that my way is best from time to time, but in my heart I know that the Lord is patiently, lovingly watching over me—in the best and the worst of times.

If you don't have the assurance that you're God's child, I urge you to seek it. All you have to do is surrender your pride, ask Jesus to forgive and accept you right now, and He will. It's that easy.

I love to hear from readers, either by e-mail, VAL@ValerieHansen.com or at P.O. Box 13, Glencoe, AR, 72539. I'll do my best to answer as soon as I can—in the meantime visit my Web site at www.ValerieHansen.com.

Blessings,

Valerie Hansen

QUESTIONS FOR DISCUSSION

1. In the beginning, Chancy blames herself for not being there to help when tragedy struck her parents. Have you ever felt negligent when you missed an opportunity to help someone? What did you do about it?

2. When bad things happen to bad people, it's easy to justify the results, but when bad things seem to overtake good people, do you think it's unfair? Why?

3. Nate works for the National Weather Forecast Service as a tornado chaser, which scares Chancy, since her parents were killed in a tornado. Are her fears unreasonable? How will her new knowledge of the inner workings of severe storms help her cope in the future?

4. Nate wants to uproot his grandparents from their beloved home and community and move them to Oklahoma to be closer to him. Have you ever been in a similar situation? How did you handle it?

5. Hester and Ted Collins, Nate's grandparents, still seem very much in love, even after many decades of marriage. Do you know any couples like them? What do you think their secrets are to a long and happy marriage?

6. Chancy hires Joanna to work in her store without asking for references or even a home address or phone number. Do you think Chancy was naive and too trusting or just eager to help a woman in need? Have you ever done anything like this? What happened?

7. Sometimes, the folks who have the strongest faith seem to be the ones who have faced the hardest trials. Do you think those trials may be part of the reason they are so strong? Why or why not?

8. After spending time with Nate, Chancy realizes that he is less certain in his faith than she is. Should she have been worried that they would be unevenly yoked in the eyes of the Lord? Or is that something to worry about later on in a relationship?

9. Chancy is a part of a close-knit Sunday school class. How can such a group add to your faith and fellowship? Discuss.

10. Nate proposes marriage to Chancy at the end of the book. Does it seem too soon for them to get engaged? Not soon enough? Why? Do you believe in love at first sight?

REQUEST YOUR FREE BOOKS!
2 FREE RIVETING INSPIRATIONAL NOVELS
PLUS 2 FREE MYSTERY GIFTS

Love Inspired®
SUSPENSE

YES! Please send me 2 FREE Love Inspired® Suspense novels and my 2 FREE mystery gifts. After receiving them, if I don't wish to receive any more books, I can return the shipping statement marked "cancel." If I don't cancel, I will receive 4 brand-new novels every month and be billed just $3.99 per book in the U.S. or $4.74 per book in Canada, plus 25¢ shipping and handling per book and applicable taxes, if any*. That's a savings of 20% off the cover price! I understand that accepting the 2 free books and gifts places me under no obligation to buy anything. I can always return a shipment and cancel at any time. Even if I never buy another book from Steeple Hill, the two free books and gifts are mine to keep forever.

123 IDN EL5H   323 IDN ELQH

Name   (PLEASE PRINT)

Address   Apt. #

City   State/Prov.   Zip/Postal Code

Signature (if under 18, a parent or guardian must sign)

Order online at www.LoveInspiredSuspense.com
Or mail to Steeple Hill Reader Service™:
IN U.S.A.: P.O. Box 1867, Buffalo, NY 14240-1867
IN CANADA: P.O. Box 609, Fort Erie, Ontario L2A 5X3

Not valid to current Love Inspired Suspense subscribers.

Want to try two free books from another series?
Call 1-800-873-8635 or visit www.morefreebooks.com

* Terms and prices subject to change without notice. NY residents add applicable sales tax. Canadian residents will be charged applicable provincial taxes and GST. This offer is limited to one order per household. All orders subject to approval. Credit or debit balances in a customer's account(s) may be offset by any other outstanding balance owed by or to the customer. Please allow 4 to 6 weeks for delivery.

Your Privacy: Steeple Hill is committed to protecting your privacy. Our Privacy Policy is available online at www.eHarlequin.com or upon request from the Reader Service. From time to time we make our lists of customers available to reputable firms who may have a product or service of interest to you. If you would prefer we not share your name and address, please check here. ☐

LISUS07

Love Inspired®
SUSPENSE

TITLES AVAILABLE NEXT MONTH
Don't miss these four stories in July

NO LOVE LOST by Lynn Bulock
Cozy mystery

She married a murderer? Gracie Lee Harris was sure Hal, her ex-husband, didn't have *that* dark a side. But with her ex as the prime suspect in his fiancée's death and her boyfriend, Ray Fernandez, as the lead investigator, Gracie could only pray that Hal's secrets wouldn't get *her* killed!

DEATH BENEFITS by Hannah Alexander
A HIDEAWAY novel

Attending a wedding in Hawaii seemed the perfect tropical dream to Ginger Carpenter...until an escaped convict began stalking her young foster nieces. To protect them, she would have to rely on Dr. Ray Clyde—the one man she never wanted to see again.

VALLEY OF SHADOWS by Shirlee McCoy
A LAKEVIEW novel

Heartbroken following the death of her nephew, the last thing Miranda Shelton expected was to become involved in a DEA investigation. Yet now she and Agent Hawke Morran were running for their lives, desperate to uncover the truth behind the betrayal that brought them together.

DANGEROUS SECRETS by Lyn Cote
Harbor Intrigue

The town of Winfield's peacefulness was shattered by the bizarre death of Sylvie Patterson's cousin. And as the last person to see him alive, Sylvie was square in the sights of investigator Ridge Matthews. But as another family member died and Ridge got closer to the truth, they must learn to trust in each other—and God—to uncover the deadly secrets lurking in her once quiet town.

LISCNM0607